THE SERGEANT MAJOR'S DAUGHTER

Sheila Walsh

When young Felicity Vale became orphaned and impoverished and had to accept her cousin's grudging help, life seemed pretty bleak. Lord Stayne, master of Cheynings, knew exactly what a woman's role in Regency England was; Captain Hardman had his own plans for Felicity; and even the six-year-old heir was determined to make life miserable for her. But Felicity had wit, wiles and beauty as her weapons and she put them to good use in finding happiness – and in teaching Lord Stayne how wrong he was!

SHEILA WALSH

The Sergeant Major's Daughter

John Curley & Associates, Inc.
South Yarmouth, Ma.

Library of Congress Cataloging in Publication Data

Walsh, Sheila.
    The Sergeant Major's daughter.

    (A Regency romance)
    Large print ed.
    1. Large type books. I. Title. II. Series:
Regency romance.
[PS3573.A47225S4 1981]   813'.54   80-26801
ISBN 0-89340-310-5

Copyright © 1977 by Sheila Walsh

Published in Large Print by arrangement with Georges
Borchardt, Inc., New York.

Distributed in the U.K. and Commonwealth by Magna Print
Books.

Printed in Great Britain

The Sergeant Major's Daughter

Chapter One

The northbound stage rumbled from the yard of the Swan Inn and plunged into the teeming congestion of Stapleforth's main thoroughfare. The driver whipped up the horses and to the accompaniment of much cursing and shouting cleared himself a path. In a remarkably short space of time the coach was free of the town and swaying perilously along between high Wiltshire hedges.

Some five miles were covered in this manner before the road widened suddenly. The coach lumbered to a halt. The driver swung his bulk nimbly to the ground, his stentorian boom advising the inside passengers that this was where the young lady was wishful to be set down.

Felicity Vale restored the sleeping baby with infinite care to the arms of its mother and set about collecting up her

1

gloves and her reticule. Then there were friendly farewells to be exchanged all around, for the remaining passengers had quite taken to the vital, long-legged girl whose lively conversation had done so much to relieve the tedium of their journey.

Much later, when they were hard put to it to describe her, they would recall a mouth which quirked often into rueful laughter as she talked, and a skin so brown as to make her eyes shine out like twin jewels. And her stories!

Such stories she had told them of her travels – of splendid cities and barren plains, of great disasters and greater victories – and of that last and greatest victory of them all when "Boney" had finally been beaten and how the great Duke himself had actually spoken to her! There had been a sadness behind the eyes as she talked – some personal tragedy they guessed from her dress, though to be sure she was not alone in that; hardly a family in the land had emerged unscathed from the long years of war.

Good wishes were echoing in her ears as Felicity picked up the small guitar from the corner, slung it across her shoulder by its strap, and leaped lightly down from the coach.

The driver had extricated from the bulging boot a small, shabby portmanteau which contained the few of her possessions not packed into the single corded trunk and left back at the Swan Inn.

He eyed her doubtfully as she took it and jerked his head toward the massive crested gates set back at an angle from the road.

"That's your direction, missy," he wheezed. "But you've a tidy step afore you and no mistake. I still say as you'd have done better to've hired yourself a gig or somesuch in Stapleforth."

"Goodness – I am not afraid of a little exercise." Felicity laughed and held out her hand to him. "Indeed, I shall enjoy it after sitting for so long. But you have been very kind and I thank you for it."

She forbore to add that her purse would not run to the hiring of gigs and that she had no wish to arrive at her cousin's door already in debt. Indeed, the tip for the driver was less than his kindness merited, but she hoped that the warmth of her thanks would compensate.

She waved the coach from sight before turning with determined cheerfulness toward those imposing gates, thrown open to invite exploration of the long, shady avenue of elms beyond. A small gatehouse appeared empty, so with no one to direct her she began to walk.

More than a half hour later she was still walking, lingering from time to time where a break in the line of trees or hedgerow disclosed some particular view of breathtaking beauty.

In all her journeyings there had been nothing to equal England in summer. She was still not quite used to so much green – or so much variety of landscape crammed into every mile. The carriageway meandered gracefully until, with a disconcerting final twist, all was changed.

Felicity stood – and stared.

Ahead of her stretched a wide, straight walk, sentineled by poplars of exact height and shape, fanning out in the distance to expose to view a building which, even from where she stood, exuded a grotesque air of grandeur.

"Glory!" she exclaimed aloud. "I must have missed the way! Amaryllis can't be living in that great barracks of a place!"

A scythe moving rhythmically in the meadow behind her hovered in its downward sweep and an uncertain voice said, "Beg pardon, ma'am?"

Felicity swung around as a wrinkled face loomed over the hedge.

"Oh, thank goodness!" She smiled at the old man. "Would you be so good as to tell me if the house beyond is Cheynings?"

"Ah, it be."

She was disconcerted. "Then perhaps there is another house of that name?"

The gardener sniffed. "Only one Cheynings, ma'am. That's been the home of the Earls of Stayne right back to

5

King Henry VIII, that has. 'Course it's changed a mite since. They've all 'ad a go at it over the years, and a right skimble-skamble job they made of it!"

Hastily curtailing this architectural homily, Felicity asked, "Do you know if a Mrs. Delamere lives there?"

"Ah. Poor little widow woman. That was Master Antony's bride, that was ... and a bonnier creature I never did see. She and the boy have been here more'n a twelvemonth, now ... since Master Antony was took ... " He shook his head and muttered to himself.

Felicity thanked him and bade him good day, hiding her dismay. Of course, Amaryllis had married a younger son, but she had not supposed her to be living in such splendor.

First instincts favored instant flight, but the disciplines of an army upbringing would not permit such conduct ... and, anyway, where would she go?

Closer inspection of the building bore out the gardener's censure. The centerpiece was unmistakably Tudor and quite delightful, but the rest was a sprawling hodgepodge of styles reaching the height of absurdity in a pseudo-Eastern temple!

The young footman who answered the pealing bell goggled at the swarthy young Amazon – five feet ten inches in her stocking feet – and, observing the guitar and shabby bag, was about to send her packing as an itinerant gypsy when the smooth-faced butler appeared at his shoulder.

A man of much greater discernment, Cavanah looked beyond the superficial to the undoubted quality in the steady gray-green eyes, where lurked a humorous appreciation of the situation.

Miss Vale was ushered into a medieval hall of awe-inspiring proportions. She exclaimed aloud and the butler permitted himself a smile.

"Ah, yes, madam – we are famous for our hall. A very fine example of hammer beams – one of the finest in the country, we are reliably informed."

Felicity hid a smile and duly admired the hammer beams. Famous the hall

might be; confoundedly drafty it certainly was! She noticed that they kept two
fires burning though the day was warm.
Her eye was drawn to the grand sweep of
the staircase; a young man, undoubtedly a Corinthian of the first stare, had
paused in the moment of ascending to
put up his glass.

The odious familiarity of his scrutiny
brought a dangerous sparkle to her eyes
as he inclined his head and sauntered on
his way.

"Who is that?" Felicity asked
abruptly.

"The gentleman is Mr. Tristram Dytton – one of Madam's guests," Cavanah
replied smoothly. No mere milk-and-
water miss, this cousin of Mrs. Antony's
– a young lady to be reckoned with, or he
missed his guess.

When she was presently shown into
the drawing-room, Felicity was dis-
mayed to find her cousin not alone. Reluctantly she stepped forward, her feet
sinking into deep blue carpet; against a
blackcloth of rose damask many pairs of

eyes followed her progress, brows arched in amused interest.

Among the gentlemen present was the Corinthian she had encountered earlier. He was shorter than he had seemed on the staircase, which made the yellow pantaloons and tightly waisted coat seem the more absurd. Above the complex folds of his cravat he inclined his head in a gesture of recognition; his remark, addressed to the lady at his side, reached Felicity distinctly.

"Did I not say? Bwown as a nut, egad! But such a figure! A Juno, m'dear – a vewitable Juno!"

A faint titter came from somewhere in the room. Felicity was made desperately aware of her inches – and of the travel-crumpled black dress and the stain upon her spencer where the fat lady's baby had dribbled down it.

Her eyes sparked momentarily and then moved to seek out the beautiful, indolent creature who reclined upon a nearby sofa. Eyes like gentian violets opening to the sun widened in response to the huskily voiced greeting.

"Lud!" the vision exclaimed, her incredulous glance flicking over Felicity. "Are you in truth my cousin? How you have grown! I declare I should never have known you."

This droll observation brought a further titter and Felicity, coloring slightly, was forced to take a firm hold on her temper. For her, there was no problem of recognition.

Amaryllis had been a pretty child; as a woman she was breathtakingly lovely. A flawless skin rivaling the delicate bloom of magnolias was enhanced by black, silken curls; if the eyes were a little hard and the rosebud mouth pursed with discontent, these were but small imperfections.

Her manners, however, were less impressive, though Felicity was obliged to acknowledge that tiredness was probably making her oversensitive. It was perfectly understandable that Amaryllis should appear a trifle cool. To be suddenly confronted by a relative whose existence was but indifferently known to one was bound to be something of a facer.

She resolved to set matters straight.

"I am obviously not expected," she said with some crispness. "I have no wish to impose myself upon you, cousin. Clearly my letter has gone astray."

Amaryllis asked with conspicuous reluctance, "Are my . . . are your parents also back in England?"

"They are both dead." The bleakness of the reply was echoed in Felicity's eyes. A tiny, involuntary ripple of shock ran around the room, but she was unaware of it as she knew again the despair of total bereavement. It was in part this despair which had led her to seek out her sole remaining family, for did not blood call to blood at such a time?

To be sure, they had met no more than a few times – and that as children – but had not Amaryllis herself lost husband and mother over recent months? It should have forged a bond between them. Watching Amaryllis now, pettishly plucking at the fine, floating gown of deepest violet, which so exactly mirrored her eyes – and seeing in those eyes an ill-concealed relief that she would not be called upon to receive an aunt and uncle whom she despised – Felicity was forced to acknowledge that her judgment had been sadly out.

"Well, I am very sorry to be sure," Amaryllis was saying. "I suppose since you are here, you had best remain – for the present, at any rate."

Dear God! Does she imagine I am come to sponge on her? Felicity's spirit moved in revolt.

"No. I will not stay," she said quickly. "I came only ... " Here she stopped. Only to enlist your aid in securing me a position, was what she had intended to say, but before so many people – and with that odious man's glass upon her – the words stuck, and with craven cowardice she allowed them to remain unspoken.

"I see now that it was foolish of me to come as I did. I have left a trunk at the

12

Swan in Stapleforth. If you will provide me with some form of conveyance, I will trouble you no further, cousin."

"Bwavo! Well spoken, Juno!" applauded the Corinthian. "Amawyllis – you'll not let this so charming cousin escape?"

Amaryllis wriggled her shoulders. "Oh, for goodness' sake! I have said she may stay, have I not?" She turned impatiently to Felicity. "You cannot possibly put up at a common hostelry alone."

The absurdity of this was too much for Felicity. Why should she care for the good opinion of these people? Her good humor restored, she said with a twinkle, "My dear Amaryllis, you would be amazed at some of the places I have been thankful to lay my head. No, my difficulties are, I fear, financial. Not to put too fine a point on it, coz, I have scarcely a feather to fly with and must secure a position without delay. I thought perhaps a governess – or a companion – I believe I have the necessary skills. It occurred to me that you might know of someone – a personal recommendation would undoubtedly carry more weight."

There – it was out! The various reactions were fascinating to behold. Amaryllis flushed bright red, furious, Felicity supposed, at being so let down before her friends; the friends tried to look as though they hadn't heard ... except for Mr. Dytton, who studied her anew – and with a subtle shift in the degree of familiarity. She knew without a doubt that there would be many Mr. Tristram Dyttons in her life from now on; the prospect depressed her beyond measure.

Amaryllis had recovered sufficiently to manage a brittle laugh. "Lud! Do not speak to me of governesses! I have just dismissed my third – and my darling Jamie scarcely more than a babe. I am nearly demented. The Earl is threatening him with the advent of a tutor, which is absurd! He is not yet seven and a most delicate child! I have the greatest difficulty in securing anyone who fully understands his needs, and am frequently left with only his father's old nurse . . . "

A calculating look passed fleetingly across her face. "Perhaps your arrival is opportune, after all."

Felicity swallowed her dismay. It was certainly no part of her plan to become an unpaid skivvy – trapped forever as a poor relation! But just for a week or two, would it be so bad? A breathing space – time to adjust her ideas and, if necessary, advertise. The bleakness of the alternative, with its inevitable depletion of her resources, decided her.

"Very well," she said. "I will stay and look after your son, cousin, but only until you are able to find a permanent replacement."

Chapter Two

Felicity tied the ribbons of the plain, dark bonnet firmly beneath her chin and drew on the fringed black silk shawl that had been her mother's. Outside her bed-chamber, she paused, then moved to the next door and soundlessly turned the handle. Jamie lay sprawled upon his bed, his dark curls spilling across the pillow, one arm outflung in sleep; beside the fireplace Nurse nodded in her comfortable chair, snoring in gentle rhythm.

The corners of her lively mouth turned upward at the sight. Felicity withdrew and directed her steps down a short, steep flight of stairs from the nursery apartments, through a bewildering maze of corridors which had once defeated her, as they had defeated many a visiting gentleman's gentleman, down more stairs, across the Long Gallery where generations of Delamere ancestors followed her progress with haughty eyes, and so to the West Wing and yet more stairs, little used except by the servants.

In this way she hoped to avoid meeting any of the house guests, an act of cowardice which she acknowledged with a rueful grimace.

On attaining the ground floor, she again skirted the main body of the house, taking instead a passage which led from the library past the armory and the muniment room and so out onto the terrace where the oppressive furnace of the August sun met her like a wall.

Not a breath stirred the great cedar tree which dominated the lawns to the rear of the house. Felicity stood, awed even now by the vista of parklands stretching into infinity. Ahead, lawns of incredible green, smooth as velvet, sloped gently toward a distant glint of water, flanked by Home Wood, where she would find a respite from the sun's glare.

Behind her as she wandered rose the

turreted walls of Cheynings; with a faint smile she recalled her first sight of its West Front. Now, in only two weeks, she had developed quite a fondness for its ugly, sprawling bulk.

Her thoughts turned to Jamie. He had proved to be less of a little horror than she had feared. He was precocious certainly, but no more than was inevitable in a six-year-old with an overdoting mamma and lacking a father's disciplining influence.

The Earl, his uncle and guardian, whose heir he now was, should have supplied the deficiency, but apart from demanding that he live at Cheynings and threatening him with advent of a tutor, he appeared to have taken little more than a perfunctory interest in the boy. The governesses who had fallen by the wayside, had been duped by Jamie into letting him do much as he pleased.

In the schoolroom on their first morning together he had eyed Felicity speculatively. "I don't feel very well," he ventured.

She looked suitably grave. "Oh dear, I am sorry. Perhaps you should return to bed and we will call the doctor."

Jamie said quickly, "I don't feel as not well as that."

"Ah. Then I suggest that we work for an hour or so. I find work a very good cure for a fit of the blue devils."

Jamie watched her take out the books. "My governesses never stay very long. They don't like it when I scream."

"No," said Felicity briskly. "I don't suppose I shall like it either – in fact, I might be tempted to do something about it." She smiled. "Is it not fortunate that I am your cousin, and not such a gudgeon as to balk at the first obstacle?"

"I am v-very delicate, you know," he stammered, clutching at fast vanishing straws.

"Yes, I know," Felicity sympathized. "It is a great pity, for I had such splendid adventures lined up for us."

"W-what sort of things?"

"Oh – well, it is of no consequence now. Perhaps when you are stronger . . .

if I am still here by then, of course. We will try page ten in your reader, if you are ready."

It was the end of Jamie's small rebellion. The two soon became fast friends. It quickly became apparent that Jamie desperately craved affection – and more than that – male approbation. Felicity discovered that he had been seeking it where he could, from the Earl's estate manager down to the gardener's boy . . . everywhere, in fact, except the stables.

"I don't like horses," he had told Felicity defensively.

More of Amaryllis's influence! The thought made her angry, but she only said casually that of course she had grown up with horses . . . and went on to regale him with splendidly hair-raising tales of battles and of a life spent following the drum.

Felicity's life had been lived among soldiers – some of them little more than boys – and she suspected that boys were much the same the world over. Hadn't her father's maxim been that they learned the sooner by example? And they all loved a good story! So she talked and Jamie listened in awe – and, she hoped, benefited.

Deep in thought, she crossed the little ornate bridge which spanned the narrow end of the lake, out of the relentless heat into the quiet coppice of beech and oak fringing the Home Wood.

Ah, that was better. Here was coolness – quivering shadows of deep, velvety browns and greens, shot through with occasional brilliant sunlight. The fronds of bracken were pungently sweet as she brushed past them, drawn onward by the whispers of a hidden stream. It proved little more than a trickle, but she flopped down beside it, grateful for the opportunity to ease the sticking muslin from her shoulders – wishing she could as easily shrug off the unaccountable depression which dogged her.

"Felicity Vale – you have much to be thankful for," she rebuked herself sternly – and sighed. It must be the oppressiveness of the weather . . . as stifling and uncomfortable as it had been in Brussels in June.

Thunder rumbled with distant menace.

There had been thunder then, too . . . it had mingled with the sound of the guns . . . and Mamma had stirred fretfully and cried out . . .

Felicity sprang to her feet, determined to shake off the morbid trend of her thoughts. The dampness of her dress had turned chill in the shade. She drew her shawl closer and hurried on.

Heavy clouds were building up behind the solid flank of the trees. There would be a storm before long; perhaps it would be prudent not to linger. Still preoccupied, she crossed the field to the wicket gate set in the thick hawthorn hedge.

She stepped into the main carriageway at the precise moment that a high-flying phaeton swept into view, driven at a bruising pace by a formidable figure in a voluminous driving coat.

Felicity was afforded a brief, terrifying glimpse of four snorting grays hurtling down upon her in the instant before she sprang for the safety of the hedge.

In happier circumstances she might have applauded the speed and competence with which the phaeton's owner dragged his team to the off and brought them to a plunging standstill. As matters were, she was fully occupied in extricating the more painful thorns from her flesh while simultaneously attempting to check her slide toward the slime of the ditch.

By the time she had ordered her scattered wits, the gentleman had thrown down his reins, ordered his tiger to the wheelers' heads, and was towering above her.

"What, in the devil's name, do you suppose you are about?" a harsh voice, clipped with rage, was demanding of her. "Have you no more sense than to step into the road without first looking where you are going?"

Felicity glared up, a long way it seemed, into black eyes narrowed to angry points of light beneath a curling hat brim; a lean, unprepossessing face, long-nosed, with the skin pulled tight, showed a faint puckered scar across the right cheekbone.

Unused to being dwarfed, she scrambled inelegantly until she had secured a firm foothold and stood – scratched by brambles, her bonnet askew, her dignity bruised, and her own temper in shreds.

"If we are to speak of sense, sir – then it is a great pity you have not the sense to drive with a little more care and con-sideration for other road-users instead of flaunting your mastery of the ribbons like some swell dragsman showing off his paces to the hoi-polloi!"

The young tiger's mouth dropped open on hearing his master's skill so abused – and him known the length and breadth of the land to be an unparal-leled whip!

The black eyes narrowed still further as the gentleman swiftly revised his opin-ion. This was no common serving

24

wench. Subjecting her to a closer scrutiny, he was treated in return to a scorching glare from gray-green eyes, thickly fringed and flecked with angry yellow specks of light. No servant had ever looked at him so! No lady, either!

"My good woman," he snapped, "it is entirely due to my mastery of the ribbons that you are not this instant lying mangled beneath my horses' hooves – which is precisely where you deserve to be!"

Insolent creature – to stand so while she struggled to free the fringe of her shawl, which had become inextricably tangled in the brambles. But no more than one would expect of Amaryllis's friends!

"Sir!" she returned in quivering tones. "I am not your good woman!"

"No, by God! If you were, you would have been better schooled to mind your manners. Permit me." With infuriating, frigid politeness he leaned forward and released her errant shawl.

Felicity drew it around her shoulders

and stepped across the ditch away from him.

"One moment, madam."

She half turned, meeting his lowering glance with icy civility.

"You will oblige me by telling me who you are – and by what right you are using these grounds."

"I do not see how it can possibly concern you, sir – but since you ask, I am residing at Cheynings."

With this lofty speech she turned on her heel and marched away up the drive.

The gentleman watched her straight-backed retreat. "The devil you are!" he breathed.

Felicity heard him command the tiger to let the horses go. A moment later the phaeton flashed past her, the driver sparing her not so much as a glance.

Temper sustained her until, climbing to the haven of her own bedchamber, she flung off bonnet and shawl and sat down heavily upon the dressing stool, resting her chin in her hands to contemplate her reflection in the tiny, inadequate mirror. An unfashionable glow in her cheeks lent added brilliance to her snapping eyes ... the sight brought laughter bubbling up.

Oh, why had she admitted to staying here? That wretched creature would assuredly complain to Amaryllis and the culprit would be easily identified, since none of her cousin's guests, to her knowledge, was of more than average height, or affected dark gray muslin and wore her hair severely drawn back under a plain dark bonnet.

Felicity touched her hair regretfully; her nose was uncompromisingly short and straight, her chin had often been termed stubborn, but her hair had been her one claim to distinction – like ripe horse chestnuts, Papa was used to describe it with affectionate pride – and she had worn it so prettily dressed. But such vanities were not for would-be governesses and so she had devised a neat, if unbecoming knot with just a softening fringe across her brow.

These ruminations came to an abrupt

end as the door was flung open. Not for the first time Felicity stifled annoyance that Amaryllis did not even accord her the courtesy of knocking before entering her room.

Her cousin wore a pettish look which made Felicity fear the worst. She flounced across to the bed and spread the skirts of a new sprig muslin dress. Her opening words, however, were unexpected.

"The most provoking thing! Maxim is arrived – quite without warning! He was to have been away a further week."

"Maxim?"

"The Earl – my brother-in-law! I declare it is monstrous inconsiderate of him to come unannounced in this way."

Felicity was amused. "Presumably, since this is his home, he must fancy himself entitled to use it as he pleases."

"Oh, Maxim always does exactly as he pleases," Amaryllis declared waspishly. "The feelings of others never concern him overmuch, as you will discover. You are to present yourself at once in the library." Felicity knew a sudden, quite inexplicable unease. "Something has put him in a vastly disagreeable mood," Amaryllis continued. "So pray do not keep him waiting or we shall all be the sufferers. My weekend party is already likely to be ruined!"

The unease was fast turning to awful premonition.

"Amaryllis? Your brother-in-law? From what Jamie has said, I had supposed him to be an elderly man."

Amaryllis jumped up impatiently. "Good heavens, no! Well, of course, he was some years older than my poor Antony – and his hair is gone quite gray – but he is not old, precisely."

"And does he drive a team of high-colored grays?"

"I believe I have seen him do so," came the careless reply. "He is a noted whip I am told, as well as being a bruising rider. Indeed, I am dreading the day when he will insist upon Jamie's learning to ride. The poor lamb is quite terrified."

Such an admission would normally

have roused Felicity to indignation; now, she scarcely heard. Oh, good God! she thought. I am undone!

"You had best bring Jamie downstairs with you," Amaryllis concluded, insensitive as ever to the effect her words had produced. "Maxim will surely wish to see him ... and he may come to me while you talk. And do hurry!"

Felicity had time to do little more than wash and change her lace collar for a clean one – and to stem Jamie's chatter for long enough to ensure that he was presentable.

At the door of the library she rubbed the palms of her hands against her skirts.

"Are you nervous, Cousin F'licity?" Jamie asked with ghoulish interest.

"Of course not!" she asserted and took his hand.

The room was full of dark wainscoting and heavy furniture and was lined from floor to ceiling with books.

The figure standing at the window with his back to them was very tall. The sunlight turned his hair to silver – and in the instant before he turned, one half of Felicity's mind was able calmly to approve the set of the olive-green coat across broad shoulders, while the other half quaked in the certain knowledge that when he did turn, there would be a scar running across his right cheekbone.

It was almost a relief to have her expectation confirmed. The eyes, she discovered, were not black, but a chilling slate gray.

She managed a tolerable composure as Amaryllis performed brief introductions. The Earl's coldness of manner and general air of hauteur were not encouraging, but she was determined not to be cast down.

Jamie, to her surprise, overcame his awe to fling himself upon his uncle, tugging imperatively at his pale, buff breeches. The Earl, who had frowned on seeing the child, removed him at once to a safe distance and desired him to contain his enthusiasm – and his sticky fingers.

Jamie muttered reproachfully. "My

fingers are not sticky! Cousin F'licity made me wash them – twice!"

The double injustice obviously rankled. There might have been the suspicion of a glint in the Earl's eye as he commanded Jamie nevertheless to do as he was bid – and to go with his mamma onto the terrace. There was no sign of it, however, when he turned his attention back to Felicity.

In total silence she endured a cold, inquisitorial inspection from top to toe.

"So, Miss Vale," he said at last in that harsh voice, "you wish to become a governess?"

"Not precisely, my lord," she amended, half humorously. "It would be truer to say that necessity has forced the decision upon me."

"A nice distinction, ma'am. I shall bear it in mind." His mouth thinned. "Permit me to inform you, however, that from our admittedly brief acquaintance, I can conceive of no one less suited to hold such a position."

Her chin rose consideringly. "Really,

my lord? And is it your custom always to formulate such damning opinions on the basis of one unfortunate encounter? I cannot believe it possible."

"Can you not, Miss Vale?" His eyes were turning black again. "Then you force me to speak more plainly. I trust you will acquit me of mere prejudice when I state, as I must, that every word you utter confirms me in my opinion. There is a lack of deference, a want of docility in your general demeanor which must alienate any would-be employer at the outset."

Felicity flushed and bit her lip.

"However," he added with gentle malice, "you are fortunate, are you not, in finding a kinswoman gullible enough to take you in and permit you to practice your ... skills ... upon her offspring."

"I am indebted to Amaryllis, of course." The effort of holding down her temper made Felicity's voice shake slightly. "But it has never been my intention to accept her hospitality ... " Here she broke off in some confusion.

He inclined his head as she concluded defiantly, " ... I daresay I should say your hospitality, Lord Stayne, for one moment longer than I must!"

"Pride, too, Miss Vale?" His voice was now decidedly mocking her. "It really won't do, you know."

Clutching at the tattered rags of her good intentions, she swallowed the retort which rose to her lips and even managed an abrupt laugh.

"You are a harsh critic, sir. I see it will be of little use ever to apply to you for a character reference. If my faults are indeed as numerous and as damning as you infer – then I must strive to mend them with all speed – for I am determined to support myself as soon as Amaryllis can replace me."

"Then I shall raise no objection to your remaining for the present." The Earl's ironic gaze moved to the terrace where Amaryllis could be heard plaintively entreating her precious not to make his mamma's head ache.

"It has for some time been my intention to engage a tutor for Jamie. I have a young man in mind – a clergyman, at present bear-leading the son of a friend of mine around Rome. In the meantime, I doubt you can make a worse job of controlling my nephew than his mother and that hapless band of nonentities have so far achieved!"

With which damning encomium he gave her a brief nod of dismissal and moved toward the terrace, signaling Jamie to go with Miss Vale.

Stiff-rumped, long-nosed bastard! fumed Felicity, with all the unladylike candor of her army upbringing. From his chatter, however, she deduced that Jamie did not share her opinion. Despite the fact that to her eyes his manner appeared harsh, demanding as it did instant obedience, Jamie held his magnificent relative in awed esteem. She could only suppose it stemmed from his total deprivation of any kind of masculine idol.

That evening, as usual, she took supper on a tray in her room. The question had never been broached, but Felicity could not suppose that her presence would be welcome downstairs. For her part she was not sorry; she found her cousin's friends, almost without exception, empty-headed and boring.

But for once even Mrs. Hudson's cooking did not tempt her. Finally she pushed the tray aside and collected her shawl. Outside it was growing dark much earlier than usual. Thunder rumbled constantly in the distance and there was a stifling, unnatural stillness – like those June days in Brussels...

She had been fighting it off all day, this sense of oppression; now, in the gathering dusk she gave it full rein. Light streamed from the windows of Cheynings... like the Duchess of Richmond's house on the night of the ball...

Felicity, sitting at her mother's bedside, had heard the Colonel and Mrs. Patterson come home early and shortly afterward the slam of the front door. A few whispered words with Mrs. Patterson had confirmed that the Colonel

36

had gone to join his regiment. The army was moving out. Napoleon had crossed the Sambre and had thrown the whole weight of his army against the Prussians.

"The Duke came to the ball, my dear," Mrs. Patterson had told her. "I think it quite splendid of him, when he must have had so much on his mind, for if he had not done so, most of those stupid people would have panicked – you know how matters have been here in Brussels these past days – so many rumors! Alastair says the French have taken Charleroi . . . the situation is grave."

Felicity's thoughts had flown instantly to her father. She had wondered where he was, as through the long night she sat with the casements thrown wide against the heat, listening to the familiar sound of the drums beating to arms. If she shut her eyes she could hear them yet – or was it only the thunder?

When her mother finally slept, she had crept out into the Place Royale to watch as she had watched so many times . . .

37

even now she could recall with heightened sensation every sight, every smell, every sound which had disturbed that airless dawn . . . the ever-beating drums, enforced by the occasional summoning note of a bugle . . . gun-carriages rumbling into position . . . and the smell of sweating horses, their harnesses creaking and jingling as they stamped the echoing cobbles.

And everywhere the friendly voices followed her as she had picked her way past the loaded commissariat trains, between corn bags and horse-feed bags and all the paraphernalia of an army moving into action.

Men were tumbling into the square from all directions, shakos askew, pulling on jackets as they came – some carrying children, with wives running at their sides – some alone. Young boys looking lost and apprehensive . . . and old-timers for whom it was just another battle.

"Come to bid us farewell, have you, lassie?" grinned a burly rifleman, whistling through his teeth as he lovingly polished an already gleaming rifle. She had stayed among them until the lines began to form up in the paling light from the east.

And then the regiments were moving toward the Namur Gate, laughing and joking, their steady rhythmic tramp shaking the ground – and dear, funny old General Picton riding ahead of them with his top hat and his frockcoat, and his spyglass hung about his neck, calling cheerily to friends who lined the way and waving to the stolid, incurious Flemish folk coming into the city with their wagons of vegetables.

By four o'clock the sun was up, hurting her eyes as it flashed off sword-hilt and bayonet – picking out vividly the swaying scarlet phalanx of the infantry and the green-jacketed riflemen – the blue-coated Belgians and the Brunswickers in their black – and the gallant Highlanders, their kilts swinging to the skirl of the pipes ...

And then they were gone ... out along the Charleroi road ... the sounds dying away to mingle with the distant gun-fire . . .

Felicity had been sitting crouched upon a corner of the terracing which traversed the rose garden. She rose, cramped and stiff, and found her cheeks wet with tears. Impatiently, she brushed them away; looking back was a useless exercise, after all; perhaps later, much later – when the hurt was less.

She turned with a sigh to retrace her steps – and caught a drift of cigar smoke on the still air.

"Miss Vale?"

Oh, drat the man! Felicity bit her lip in vexation as the Earl approached her across the lawn from the shadow of the cedar tree.

"Lord Stayne. I am sorry. I have disturbed your walk."

"You have not disturbed me – not in the way you mean." He stood looking down at her through a cloud of smoke and then threw away his cigar. "I have been watching you for some minutes," he went on in his abrupt way. "Tell me, are you unwell, Miss Vale?"

She averted her face, lest the lights from the house revealed too much. "No, my lord. I am quite well, I thank you."

He frowned. "I wondered. You were not at dinner."

"No, sir. I prefer to take a tray in my room."

"Prefer, Miss Vale?" he queried with gentle emphasis.

"Yes, sir. I . . . do not find myself easy in the company of my cousin's friends."

The Earl uttered an abrupt laugh. "No more do I, Miss Vale – no more do I. I cannot allow that to be sufficient reason for skulking in your room. While I am in residence, at least, you will oblige me by dining with the family."

He saw her figure stiffen and added with exaggerated courtesy, "If you please!"

Felicity nodded ungraciously and again attempted to leave.

"Miss Vale?"

"My lord?"

"Are you happy here?"

41

The question took her by surprise. Before she could frame a reply, he continued, "You do not look happy. It occurs to me that it must be quite unlike anything to which you have hitherto been accustomed."

Her already lacerated feelings were instantly rubbed raw. How dare he patronize her.

"I may have lacked a settled home, Lord Stayne," she retorted, "but I assure you my parents always managed to ensure that I lived tolerably well."

The silence stretched until she could endure it no longer; but the Earl was before her, his tone cutting.

"My dear young lady, your life style is not in question. My concern is solely that you might be experiencing a loss of companionship – a bond of family affection which you must, until recently, have enjoyed."

"Oh!" Hot color rushed into Felicity's face, unseen; she lowered her head as scalding tears locked her throat.

Stayne surveyed the bent head and

said in milder tones, "You really must strive to contain that impetuous tongue, Miss Vale. It will run you into serious trouble one day."

When she still made no move, he added testily, "I trust you are not going to treat me to tears. Amaryllis invariably uses them as the ultimate weapon, but I must say I had not thought you so poor-spirited."

Felicity swallowed hard. "Then unless you wish to be proved wrong, sir, you had best give me leave to withdraw."

"Certainly not. I have not nearly done with you. There is a great deal more I would know of your background."

Amaryllis was right! The man had not the least delicacy of feeling! She straightened up and glared at him, not caring if he saw her lashes spiked with tears.

"That is much better," he approved. "My sister-in-law has told me a little about you. Your father was a sergeant major. His regiment?"

"The 23rd Light Dragoons, my lord."

"My brother was with the 12th. He died with General Hay at the siege of Bayonne, when hostilities were all but ended."

There was that in his voice which made her feel she must have misjudged him. She said impulsively, "I'm sorry. You were close?"

"Very close." His voice was curt. "But we are not speaking of my affairs, Miss Vale. Your father was killed at Waterloo?"

Felicity's mind, still half-engulfed in searing memory, shied away. She nodded.

"And your mother?"

The thunder was rolling nearer – louder now. On the still, heavy air the scent of roses was overpowering.

"We knew she was dying," Felicity said. "The doctors could do little for her and she refused to leave my father. When she became suddenly worse, Mrs. Patterson insisted on taking her in. They had known one another a long time – were two of a kind, in fact. The Colonel

44

managed to arrange for my father to come – just for a few hours."

She could only guess what it must have cost Papa – sitting on her mother's bed, smiling, her hands clasped tightly in his – and promising in that gruff, yet gentle voice he kept only for her, "This time we'll fix 'Boney' for good, dearest – then it's back to England for us – we'll have you on your feet in no time at all . . ."

The Earl, watching her face, found it extraordinarily revealing and totally at odds with her prosaic account of events.

How many young women of his acquaintance, he wondered, would have had the stomach to stay beside a dying mother in a panic-torn city ravaged by terrible thunderstorms, the streets clogged by mud-caked fugitives and streams of wounded, while a troop of Hanoverian cavalry stormed through, scattering everything in its path and shouting that all was lost.

And for this girl all had been lost. Yet here she was telling him, with only a slight faltering in her narrative, of riding out to the battlefield with one of her father's men, to bring his body home on a handcart so that she could bury her parents together in a little local churchyard, where pink cabbage roses climbed over the walls . . .

The reality defied imagination. "A harrowing experience, Miss Vale," he said at last.

"It was not easy, but it had to be done," she said simply, her voice a little huskier than usual. Talking had been an ordeal, but it had been worthwhile; she felt empty – yet, in a curious way, released. "Afterward there were so many wounded to be cared for; it left little time for personal grief."

"But you had friends?"

"Oh yes! Many, many friends. People were unbelievably kind. The Pattersons in particular – I had stayed with them often over the years, helping with the children.

"However, with my father gone, I no longer had any place on the army's strength – nor could I accept for long the hospitality of friends, however willingly offered." She met his eyes with a shade of the old defiance. "Besides, there were too many memories."

"So?"

"I found a note from Amaryllis among Mamma's effects, telling of her own mother's death. It bore this address, so on an impulse I wrote to acquaint her with my own altered circumstances, hoping she might help me to find an agreeable situation – and set off without waiting for a reply."

In the light streaming from the windows of Cheynings the Earl's glance was, to say the least, quizzical.

"Yes, I know," she agreed ruefully. "I see now, of course, that it was an idiotish thing to do.

"As far as I could remember, Amaryllis and I had dealt tolerably together as children, though our paths seldom crossed. It was my Aunt Eugenie who couldn't stand me – a skinny brown hoyden, all arms and legs and no manners, was how she described me, as I recall – and I daresay she was right!"

To Felicity's surprise, Stayne laughed. "That sounds like Lady Whitney! I collect your mother and she were not much alike?"

"Only superficially. Both were beautiful and it was intended that they should both marry well. Aunt Eugenie duly obliged, but Mamma was less conformable. She fell in love with my father and would have no other, so they washed their hands of her."

"I see."

There was a crack of thunder quite close; the first heavy spots of rain splattered the ground. The Earl put a hand under Felicity's arm and turned her in the direction of the house.

"Tell me, Miss Vale – has Amaryllis spoken of payment?"

Felicity stumbled and his grasp tightened.

"Heavens, no! We have never discussed it, but ... no. I am grateful for the breathing space – and, truly, young

Jamie is no trouble."

"I am astonished to hear you say so. To my mind he has been most shockingly spoiled!"

"There is nothing wrong with Jamie that time and a little true affection won't mend. That – and perhaps a more regular interest taken in him by a man in whom he could repose his confidence and admiration."

Stayne glanced down at her sharply. "Are you by any chance taking me to task, young woman?"

"I am stating a simple fact, sir. A boy of Jamie's age sets great store by a man's good opinion – preferably his parent, but in Jamie's case his uncle and guardian. It is quite apparent that he holds you in high esteem; it seems a pity, therefore, that he must seek his credit elsewhere."

There was silence.

"I wonder, Miss Vale – are you a complete innocent or a clever tactician?"

"Sir?"

"No matter. Either way I stand rebuked and the diversion has taken us very neatly away from my original query."

"Lord Stayne – I beg you will leave matters as they are. I am more than grateful for a temporary roof over my head; to take payment as well would seem ... "

"Like charity, Miss Vale?" The interruption was harsh. "No such is intended. But while you continue to minister to my nephew, you will be paid accordingly."

"I shall not take your money, my lord."

"What an infernally argumentative girl you are! Well, we shall see, ma'am!"

The rain put an abrupt end to the dispute; in a sudden deluge they were obliged to retreat with undignified haste to the shelter of the main portico, where the Earl favored her with a brusque good night and departed.

Chapter Three

Dinner on the following evening was all that Felicity had anticipated. From the outset it was apparent that the company was unsure how far her presence should be acknowledged. Her kinship with Amaryllis amounted at best to that of a poor relation fulfilling the duties of a governess. They obviously thought it a very odd quirk of Stayne's to require her attendance at dinner – as did Amaryllis.

Felicity felt a certain degree of sympathy with them in their dilemma, since the Earl, having all but commanded her attendance, made not the least push to engage her interest.

In the event, it was the conversation which most effectively ostracized her, concerning as it did people and events completely unknown to her.

On the whole, the gentlemen behaved

rather better than the ladies, which aroused a wry conjecture as to their motives. She could in no way be considered above the ordinary; indeed, she was resigned to cutting a drab figure in her best black crape. Yet, even as she reminded herself sternly that she was in mourning, and was not there in order to shine, she could not suppress a stab of envy that, amid the rainbow glory of his guests only the Earl in the stark simplicity of his dark coat came anywhere near her for plainness.

So it was not her captivating beauty which caused the young tulip of fashion across the table to ogle her, or accounted for the way Mr. Tristram Dytton's knee so often brushed against hers beneath the linen cloth. Did they perhaps imagine her position sufficiently ambiguous to admit the possibility of a little "back of the stairs" dalliance? Glory – just let them try! The thought kindled a derisive sparkle in her eye, rousing the gentlemen concerned to new peaks of curiosity.

The absence of any enlivening conversation enabled Felicity to watch entranced as dishes of turbot, salmon, and whitebait, each dressed in its own spicy sauce – together with truffled capons, bowls of asparagus, and tiny new potatoes – were removed and replaced with several roast duckling, two or three assorted raised pies, and a sirloin of beef, pink and succulent – all accompanied by a staggering variety of salads, vegetables, sweets, puddings, ices, sweetmeats, and a great bowl of strawberries and other fresh fruits.

Mrs. Lipscombe, a near neighbor of the Earl's, inclined her feathered, turbaned head in Felicity's direction.

"You seem bewildered, Miss Vale." The overloud voice was patronizing in its graciousness. "You will not find better fare, anywhere, I believe, but I make no doubt you are not accustomed to such a superior table as his lordship is wont to keep."

Felicity saw the Earl's sardonic glance flick down the table to observe her reaction. Some imp of perversity prompted her to simper: "Indeed, no, ma'am. Why – when the army is on the move, our meals are often frugal to the point of digging for roots to provide a little thin broth! If we are fortunate enough to procure a rabbit, there is seldom time to cook it. Have you ever eaten raw rabbit, ma'am? It is quite tolerably pleasant, though the limbs can be stringy."

There were muttered exclamations and one or two chuckles from those acute enough to recognize and appreciate what was happening. The Earl appeared to have lost interest, but on looking closer Felicity saw his mouth twitch.

Mrs. Lipscombe was not universally popular. She had two children – a son, Torquil, the fashionable young sprig sitting opposite Felicity, and a daughter, Lucinda, a fair if slightly insipid beauty with an obstinate mouth. Lucinda was a frequent visitor to Cheynings, being friendly with Amaryllis – a friendship much fostered by her mamma, who cherished notions of seeing her daughter a Countess.

Mr. Lipscombe was insignificant. His wife, on the other hand, was not. Her features would have done credit to a well-bred mare and complemented her decided air of consequence, which derived from the nice distinction of being remotely connected with the Wellesleys.

Nor was Mrs. Lipscombe a fool. She was well aware that she was being roasted; her nostrils quivered slightly as she said, with a tinkling laugh, "My dear Miss Vale, such fare may satisfy the ordinary ranks, but I cannot think it would content my kinsman, the Duke of Wellington. I am sure I cannot count the number of times I have heard him express a partiality for good food."

Such a set-down would have silenced a more socially conscious protagonist, but Felicity had no such inhibitions; she persisted wickedly, "That may be the case at home, ma'am, but it is a different story when he is with his troops, I assure you. Many's a time his grace has sampled my broth – and even complimented me upon it."

There were more stifled chuckles. Mrs. Lipscombe flushed and turned away, making no further attempt at conversation. Felicity knew she would be made to suffer for her impertinence, but she remained unrepentant.

When the ladies retired to the drawing room, the outraged matron swept past her as though she were not there, the feathers of her turban threshing with the force of her displeasure. Felicity would have preferred to withdraw, having complied with the letter, if not the spirit of his lordship's commands, but now pride – that sin of which he had already accused her – dictated that she must remain.

She collected some needlework and took a quiet back seat. Amaryllis whispered crossly that she had better not cause any more trouble.

Presently the gentlemen rejoined the party. To Felicity's surprise, the Earl placed himself next to Lucinda Lipscombe, and when she was entreated to play upon the pianoforte, it was Stayne who turned the pages of her music for her.

Well, well! Who would have thought it!

For herself, Felicity was to be plagued yet again by the odious Mr. Dytton, who, in all the splendor of a bright green coat, spotted cravat, and striped satin waistcoat, fastened on her like a leech and would not be shifted. Under cover of the music he dropped into her ear several remarks which brought an angry flush to her cheeks and caused her to jab at her needlework with unnecessary ferocity.

During a lull in the entertainment he leaned forward to lisp fatuously, "Miss Vale – you must have something to offer us – a ditty or two you will have picked up on your twavels. Come now, you must not be bashful . . . did I not see you cawwying a guitar on the day you awwived?"

"A guitar . . . !" The word echoed around the room.

The Earl offered neither help nor entreaty as Felicity stumblingly disclaimed any talent.

"Songs a bit saucy, are they?" Mr. Dytton persisted with a smirk. "Campfire ditties, I daresay ... what? No matter. You will find us vewy bwoadminded, I give you my word!"

Felicity felt a sudden, overpowering need for air. Very much aware of her burning cheeks, she laid aside the needlework and, excusing herself a trifle incoherently, crossed to the open windows. As she passed out onto the terrace, she heard Mrs. Lipscombe exclaim triumphantly, "Farouche!"

But Felicity's ordeal was not ended; before she could reach the steps to the garden, her tormentor was beside her, a restraining arm encircling her waist. Here his lack of inches proved advantageous, enabling his lips to brush her cheek without lowering his head, and thus risking empalement on the ridiculously high starched points of his collar. The suggestions which accompanied his clumsy attempt at gallantry so incensed Felicity that she instantly seized upon the nearest object to hand, which proved to be a potted geranium. It was delivered with all the force which her limited aim could muster. Mr. Dytton swore and drew back – and as she turned to run down the steps, she saw the figure of the Earl clearly outlined against the open window. He called to her, but she would not stay to endure his censure.

It was some time later, as she tiptoed across the Long Gallery in the hope of regaining her room unnoticed, that her name was again called.

Felicity turned with a sigh. His lordship stood, arms folded, at the door of a lighted room. Above his head hung a portrait of the 4th Earl; and, placed so, the two profiles presented an uncanny similarity.

"I have been waiting for some time, Miss Vale. I knew you must come eventually." His voice was, for him, almost bland. "Tell me, has this retreat been strategically planned – or are you in disordered flight?"

His perception drew from her a brief, rueful grin. "I fear it is the latter, sir."

"Ah, so I thought. Well, Miss Vale, I must tell you, Mr. Dytton is not pleased with you. His pretty coat is quite ruined!"

"Oh dear." Felicity bit her lip. "Well, I am sorry – and if I must, I will apologize . . ."

"That will not be necessary," the Earl cut in. "Mr. Dytton has a most urgent appointment in Town; it will entail his leaving at first light. He will not be returning."

"Oh, but . . ." Now she was disconcerted. "Sir – in part the fault was mine. I lost my temper . . ." One eyebrow rose in mock disbelief. She sighed. "Yes, I am well aware of it, but you must allow some provocation. Until now, you see, I have always been used with respect by even the toughest of soldiers. I realize, of course, that in my altered circumstances I must accustom myself to endure the detestable civilities of men like Mr. Dytton, but ..."

"But not while you are beneath my roof," the Earl finished crisply.

"Amaryllis will be furious."

Stayne's tone became even crisper. "I do not run my establishments in order to accommodate my sister-in-law, madam – though it may often appear otherwise."

"No." There seemed little else to say. "Well then, my lord, I can only thank you, and bid you good night."

"One moment more, if you please." He regarded her pensively. "You will oblige me in future by not pitching my guests Banbury tales."

Felicity's cheeks were tinged with embarrassment and guilt.

"Quite so," he said. "Raw rabbit, indeed! And if Wellington has ever seen the inside of your 'broth pot,' I shall own myself very much surprised."

"Then I must surprise you, sir – for I once prepared him a broiled chicken in herbs which he complimented most highly!"

The eyebrow lifted again. "I am impressed, Miss Vale."

"Yes, well it was the only time," she conceded. "But I have often helped Mrs. Patterson to entertain . . . the Colonel's brother officers for the most part. What we were able to provide depended largely upon where we happened to be quartered, whether we could barter with the local peasants, and whether the Colonel had been able to indulge his passion for hunting or hare-coursing."

The imp and mischief were back. "But of course it was never in any way such superior fare as your lordship is wont to provide."

To her surprise, he put back his head and laughed. "I see you mean to remain impenitent to the end, Miss Vale."

"I fear so, my lord. But I will try to be more . . . conciliating in the future." She smiled philosophically.

"Then I wish you good night, ma'am."

Felicity turned to go; a faint look of

embarrassment crossed her face. "About Mr. Dytton, sir . . ." She saw him frown and rushed on, "I must apologize for . . . appropriating your potted geranium. I fear it was quite ruined."

The Earl's frown had grown quizzical. "Is that what it was? Do not, I beg you, give it another thought. I believe I have never seen a pot plant used to better effect. Good night, Miss Vale."

It was by far the most agreeable note on which they had yet parted company. In the days which followed, Stayne seemed to go out of his way to foster better relations.

Amaryllis, on the other hand, was determined to place the whole of the blame for Mr. Dytton's departure at her door.

"I cannot see why you must needs have caused a scene," she complained. "You are not usually missish. I believe you deliberately sought to encourage Tristram's attentions!"

"Then you are touched, cousin!" retorted Felicity sharply.

Rather than face eternal arguments, Felicity took to spending a great deal of time with Jamie out of doors. The weather had settled gloriously after the storms – and they passed many happy hours at the lakeside, building tree houses and fishing for tiddlers. Mrs. Hudson was cajoled into providing a large picnic basket so that they were not obliged to return to the house for a meal, and in the evening they stole back by a circuitous route to avoid being seen in their disheveled state.

Felicity's strategems were occasionally doomed to failure, however, as when the Earl strode from the bushes, a shotgun cradled across his arm. He halted to view the guilty pair – the child streaked with dirt, a jagged tear in his nanekin trousers – and Felicity in similar state, unable to conceal the damp patches in her dress.

She waited in resignation for the expected reprimand, but instead, he peered into the murky depths of Jamie's glass jar and commented with a faint smile, "If you aspire to fish, we must try you with rod and line." And he passed on his way with a brief nod.

Greatly encouraged, Felicity determined to extend their sporting activities. The next venture was cricket. Digby, the gardener's lad, fashioned a bat of sorts for Jamie and instructed them in the rudimentary skills. They took to playing on a little-frequented patch of green beyond the kitchen gardens and soon became quite adept, though Jamie was inclined to throw himself into the game with more enthusiasm than accuracy.

The day came, however, when he connected with commendable force.

"Oh, well played!" cried Felicity, as the ball disappeared over the high yew hedge.

There was a thud and a muttered ejaculation – and the ball reappeared a moment later in the competent hands of his uncle.

A guilty look flashed between the sporting pair. Under cover of tucking away a wayward strand of hair which had worked loose in the course of her exertions, Felicity tried somewhat nervously to judge the Earl's mood – but the hawklike features gave nothing away.

She endured the silent interrogation of his black stare for fully half a minute, while he tossed the ball from hand to hand.

Finally, he observed with extreme dryness, "You appear to dispense a singular brand of education, Miss Vale. No doubt it has a purpose?"

"It has, my lord," she retorted, charging in with all guns blazing. "It affords Jamie plenty of fresh air and exercise – and a basic interest in some of the pastimes a boy should pursue. We do a full hour of lessons morning and evening, which is sufficient for his mind to absorb at present."

"Uncle Max!" cried Jamie, emboldened to tug at his uncle's sleeve. "Wasn't that a capital hit?"

The Earl removed the small fingers from his silver-gray superfine.

"Capital," he agreed. "And if your aim continues so glaringly abroad you will continue to be caught out as you were just now."

Jamie, undeterred by this censure, eyed his uncle with an awe bordering on reverence. "Can you play cricket, sir?"

"Where do you imagine I got this scar, child? Your father hit me with a cricket ball when he was not much above your age. His aim wasn't much better than yours, as I recollect!"

These hitherto unimagined reminiscences had Jamie's eyes popping. "I say! Can you bowl overarm, sir? Digby says it has been forbidden at Mr. Lord's cricket ground."

Stayne frowned. "Who, pray, is Digby?"

Jamie's tone reproved him for his ignorance. "Digby is the gardener's boy. Can you, sir?"

The Earl transferred his gaze from the eager young face of his nephew to a highly entertained Felicity. Without a word he divested himself of his elegant coat and handed it to her. He walked some way off and came loping in to fling the ball down with astonishing speed. It was doubtful if Jamie even saw the ball, but he crowed with delight and went charging off into the bushes after it.

The Earl reclaimed his coat and queried softly, "Well, Miss Vale?"

In spite of the iron-gray hair curling fashionably about his ears, there was an air of boyish bravado in the challenge.

Felicity grinned broadly. "Very competent, my lord. Was it meant to prove something to me?"

"Only that I am heeding your strictures, madam – and am taking more interest in my nephew's doings." Stayne shrugged his way back into his coat. "I have requested Amaryllis to have riding clothes made ready for him. It is high time he learned to sit a horse. We begin next week."

Chapter Four

The small hand clutching Felicity's prickled with perspiration. As they neared the stable yard, it began to tremble. Felicity knew a moment of angry exasperation; all her careful preparations had been set at nought by the tears of one foolish woman.

Amaryllis justified her morbid fears, having had an elder brother most horribly maimed when his horse had fallen on him in the hunting field, but nothing could excuse the attack of near-hysterics which the sight of Jamie in his new riding clothes had precipitated.

Aware of the child's white, frightened face, Felicity had swallowed her rage in a desperate effort to salvage some of Jamie's wilting courage.

She stooped to cover her cousin's plucking fingers. "Amaryllis," she urged in a low voice, "will you not try – for Jamie's sake? I think he would not be fearful if you would encourage him a little – wish him luck! I have been taking him down to the stables each day, and he had become so much less nervous."

The tear-drenched blue gaze accused her. "Indeed, yes! I know very well that I have you to thank for this piece of treachery! You have been positively encouraging Stayne to notice the boy, have you not?"

"Amaryllis – Jamie must learn to ride."

"He is too young!"

"He is six – nearly seven. Can you not see . . . ?"

"I can see that my opinion counts for nothing where my son is concerned!" Amaryllis had snatched her hands away with a pettish air of drama. "I only pray that you may not live to regret your high-handedness."

With Jamie now totally demoralized, Felicity was forced to hurry him; even so, the Earl was in the stable yard before them. He saw them and checked his impatient stride, but it was an unfortunate start.

"Ah – at last," he said. "Come along, young man. Here is Mr. Dandy waiting."

Jamie eyed the shining new leather saddle on the patient gray cob's back – and shrank away.

Stayne frowned. "Come, Jamie," he commanded, his tone peremptory.

Felicity felt compelled to intervene. "My lord," she said quietly. "The child is frightened. Would it not be wiser to let him ... take matters more slowly?"

"No, madam – it would not. And if that is to be your attitude, then I suggest you return to the house and leave Jamie to me."

The small hand tightened convulsively in hers.

"Indeed I will not!"

"Very well. But if you are to stay, pray be silent and allow me to know what I am about."

"If you will only listen, sir ... Jamie is

71

frightened ... Amaryllis ..."

"Oh, good God!" Stayne exploded. "That boy has been smothered and indoctrinated until he is in danger of becoming a regular namby-pamby!"

"That is unjust! I have done my best to overcome his reticence, but Jamie's fear of horses has been long fostered – it cannot be eradicated in an instant." Felicity glared. "I am particularly fond of horses myself, but if I were afraid, I am sure there is nothing I should like less than being compelled to ride."

"Nonsense, said the Earl curtly, "Jamie is not afraid. Are you, lad?"

Jamie had almost forgotten his terrors in the fascination of their argument. No one argued with Uncle Max! His mamma would sometimes rail against him, but no one argued!

"Are you, Jamie?" his uncle repeated.

"N – no, sir." He didn't sound sure, but when Stayne held out a hand and again commanded him to come, he did so, with lagging step.

Felicity let him go with a smile of encouragement. While she waited, she wandered from stall to stall – a by-now familiar tour. There was no denying that his lordship kept an enviable stable. Halfway along she made her customary halt, as a bay with a white blaze on its brow pushed an inquisitive velvet nose forward.

"Oh, you are beautiful!" Felicity exclaimed, putting out a hand to be nuzzled. The mare nickered softly. There was breeding in every movement – in the proud lift and shake of the head, the way the ears pricked, the liveliness of the eye.

"Starlight has fair taken to you, ma'am," said Benson, the head groom, at her shoulder. "She's his lordship's latest – a fine mare – and a prime goer, but for all that, she's a rare handful and no mistake."

The sound of Mr. Dandy returning sent them both hurrying back to the yard. Felicity was relieved to see Jamie being lifted down, none the worse for his expedition. He turned a shining face to her.

"Did you see me, Cousin F'licity? Uncle Max says I did very well!"

She praised him warmly, aware of the Earl's mocking gaze; it said unmistakably, "I told you so!"

"And I may come again tomorrow, mayn't I, Uncle Max?"

"Certainly, child. If you do as well, you shall feed Mr. Dandy an apple." The Earl's gaze returned to Felicity. "You expressed a love of horses, Miss Vale. You ride, of course?"

"Tolerably well, my lord."

"Cousin F'licity was only two when she first sat a horse," Jamie insisted, with a mixture of pride and envy. "I told you, Uncle Max!"

"So you did, my boy." Felicity was beginning to feel uncomfortable under that sardonic eye. "Well, Miss Vale, we must find you a suitable mount. I should have thought of it sooner. Would you care to come now and choose?"

With Jamie clinging tightly to her hand, she again walked down the line of stalls – and was again drawn irresistibly to the bay mare.

"Starlight? You are ambitious, Miss Vale. Can you manage her, do you think?"

Felicity detected a note of amused skepticism and rose impulsively to the challenge.

"I believe so, sir. At any rate, I should like to try."

"Very well. You may put her through her paces."

She looked up, startled. "You mean . . . now?"

"Why not. There is no time like the present," said my lord blandly. "You do have riding dress?"

"Yes, of course, but . . ."

"Cold feet, Miss Vale?" he suggested.

"Certainly not!" she retorted with spirit. "But there is Jamie . . ."

"Nurse will cope adequately for a short time. Benson will have Starlight saddled while you deliver Jamie into her charge – and change your dress. You may have twenty minutes."

There was a curious silence when she

had left the yard. Benson, squarely built and forthright of manner, coughed and shuffled his feet.

"Beggin' your pardon, m'lord – but that Starlight is no fit mount for a lady, and I'm surprised at your countenancing such folly when there's a sweet-natured hack like Amber just waiting to be exercised."

"Doubtless I had my reasons." The Earl's manner discouraged argument.

"Well, it's courting disaster if you ask me," the groom persisted stubbornly. "A nice young lady like that!"

"I am not asking you," said my lord gently. "You are a prince among grooms, Benson – I have often remarked it, but do not be so foolish as to trade on my good opinion; I do not pay you to air your views. You will oblige me by doing as you are bid – and you may have Vulcan saddled for me."

Felicity came back into the stable yard looking confident and business-like – and inches taller in a riding habit of dark green wool. The close-fitting jacket with black frogging emphasized the junoes-que proportions of her figure. A severe, high-crowned shako in black, trimmed with the same dark green, completed her outfit, together with a pair of soft black leather gloves.

The sight of the two horses being walked by a couple of young stable hands brought an instant thrill, follow-ed by slight misgivings. On closer in-spection, the young mare displayed an uncomfortable degree of temperament; Felicity hoped she would be equal to her impulsive boast. As for that raking black hunter . . . she swung around to the Earl.

"You are riding with me, my lord?"

"Naturally, Miss Vale. You do not suppose that I would permit you to ride unaccompanied."

Was she imagining the note of fiend-ish anticipation? The suspicion that he was expecting her to make a cake of her-self put an added sparkle in her eye. She accepted his compliments on her ap-pearance with a composure she was far from feeling and allowed herself to be led to the mounting block.

Starlight greeted her in the usual way, but the moment Felicity settled into the saddle she could feel the packed-down energy waiting to erupt. She commanded the groom to let go and in the ensuing seconds forgot Stayne and all else in her efforts to thwart the mare's manifest determination to unseat her.

She was vaguely aware of faces – white blurs only at first as the horse caracoled, backing and rearing in an attempt to dislodge her; figures revolved like a crazy roundabout – Benson, granite-jawed, crouched swaying lightly on the balls of his feet, ready to spring; pop-eyed stable lads, and Stayne's young tiger, eyes bigger than the rest, shouting encouragement. But, above all, there was Stayne, tense, the scar showing lividly against one cheekbone, eyes narrowed as though gauging the exact moment he would intervene.

The mere possibility lent Felicity renewed determination. She had good, light hands and experience enough to resist the novice's trap of tightening the reins. She leaned forward, one hand grasping the mare firmly in the middle neck, petting and soothing her with soft, crooning words until, recognizing her voice, the nervous creature began to respond.

It was at this precise moment that a highly strung stable lad, against a clamor of protest, ducked in to grab at the staffle ... and the mare, thoroughly frightened, reared again with renewed ferocity.

Felicity cried out in exasperation: "For God's sake, get that idiot out from under!"

The boy was dragged away, catching a sharp blow on the head from one flailing hoof for his pains.

In the confusion, Felicity saw both Stayne and Benson move. In desperation she brought Starlight down sharply, turned her in a tight circle, and while she was still confused, drove her forward; together they streaked past the astonished company, under the archway of the stable yard, and headed out toward open country.

Once clear, Felicity gave Starlight her head, reveling in the sheer exhilaration of being on horseback once more. Presently she began to look about her. They were on a bridle path where the flying hooves raised a cloud of dust from the dry earth. It was new territory for her and a sharp bend in the path brought new problems. A tree had been recently felled and lay barring the way.

She selected a place where the larger branches had been lopped and with familiar tightening of stomach muscles, she gathered the horse together. They sailed over in joyous unison, and she laughed aloud.

The unexpected sound drifted back to Stayne as he thundered in pursuit. He rounded the bend in time to see horse and rider clear the obstacle in such perfect accord that he felt a swift stab of admiration.

He drew abreast and she turned a glowing face to him. By common assent they slowed to a steady trot.

"My compliments, Miss Vale. A masterly display by any standards."

Felicity's grin could have been termed impudent.

"Thank you, my lord. You are very kind – and generous, considering that I must have proved a sad disappointment."

"Now, why pray, should you think that?"

She looked demurely ahead, but a dimple quivered near her mouth. "Because you anticipated I would take a toss."

She saw the Earl's gloved hand tighten on the rein and turned to meet his sharp glance with a very straight one of her own.

"Oh, you may deny it if you will, sir – but I shall continue to suspect that the whole business was contrived in order to give me a set-down."

"What an extraordinarily devious mind you have, Miss Vale." Stayne's expression had grown sanguine. "I

81

should be foolish in the extreme to attempt any such stratagem with a young lady so intrepid that she has ridden with fearless courage over perilous mountain passes, through treacherous ravines; who has crossed the Douro on planks, bivouacked in the High Sierras in raging blizzards – and has fought her way gallantly through the parched heat of the Spanish plain . . ."

"Enough, sir, I beg you!" cried Felicity, in laughing, blushing confusion. "You must know Jamie has been fabricating stories!"

"Why – how is this, madam?" The eyebrow rose a little. "Am I to understand that you did none of these things?"

"No . . . that is . . . yes, of course I did," she stammered. "I daresay I may have embellished certain incidents in the telling . . . for Jamie's benefit . . ."

The eyebrow rose a little higher and she concluded with spirit, "But never, I swear, to the Gothic proportions you have just catalogued!"

To her amazement, the Earl uttered a

distinct chuckle. "At all events, Miss Vale, you would appear to have led a most extraordinary life. I wonder you can put up with our humdrum ways. Did you never miss the more conventional advantages of a settled home?"

"I don't believe I ever considered my life unusual, sir. But I know I should have found a conventional upbringing a dead bore. You can have no idea how much excitement can be derived from a life following the drum!"

Watching her enthusiasm, his glance grew quizzical. "And were you never lonely – as you grew older, perhaps?"

Felicity found the suggestion diverting. "Lonely? Glory – no! There was too much to do ever to be lonely or bored."

They had by now come to a gateway which led out into the village. She had seen it previously only as a distant cluster of cottages through the trees on her Sunday drives to church. Now she saw that it was quite idyllic, with a well and a duckpond and an even strip of green. It was larger than she had thought, for there were several houses lying back from the road in neat gardens, and on the corner of a lane leading out of the village a cottage was set apart from the rest by reason of its dilapidated appearance. Beyond ran the boundaries of some private land, heavily fenced and barred.

Felicity was amused to observe the bobbed curtsies and pulled forelocks that greeted their arrival; positively medieval! But she had to admit that everyone looked happy and well cared for. She was just wondering at the absence of children when a squealing, struggling mass of small bodies erupted onto the green ... a slight figure was being held and dragged inexorably toward the pond.

Felicity turned spontaneously to the Earl, expecting some assertion of authority, but there was only a slight frown of distaste.

The child was making no effort to resist his tormentors and none of the women seemed disposed to intervene.

Enraged by this shocking display of indifference, she tossed her rein to the Earl and slid to the ground.

She plunged into the melee, laying about her with her riding crop, scattering howling children in all directions until she reached their intended victim. He was a boy, not much older than Jamie – vacant eyes stared up at her from a flaccid face. She rounded on the other children in a fury – and they, stunned into silence by the angry whirlwind in their midst, began to get their second wind.

"You don't want to bother 'bout him, missus . . ."

" . . . won't take on 'arm, we're only goin' to tumble him in the pond . . ."

"He's a thief, miss . . . can't keep 'is hands to hisself . . ."

Felicity shouted at them to be silent and, in astonishment, they complied. "You should be ashamed!"

A new voice at her shoulder said quietly, "Thank you, madam. It was good of you to trouble, but it happens all the time."

Felicity turned to meet light blue eyes filled with dull resignation. She was a slight woman, pale-haired, pale-skinned, and much too thin; the bones of her skin were sharply etched – yet she was well-spoken. She carried a young baby in her arms.

"The boy is yours?"

The woman nodded. "He isn't right in the head," she explained without emotion. "He doesn't mean to steal, but when he sees something he wants, he just takes it."

"Good morning, Ester. Trouble?"

Unnoticed, the Earl had dismounted and come to join them. The woman bobbed him a curtsy as the others had done, but there was no trace of servility in the small courtesy.

"No more than usual, my lord."

He inclined his head toward the neglected cottage. "Your fence is down again, I see."

"Yes." There was tiredness in the

word. "The hens got out. It's taken me most of the morning to collect them."

"You need to get it fixed quickly, then." The Earl gestured with his whip. "That chimney looks none too safe."

The woman cast an anxious eye over the cottage roof – and sighed. "Thank you, my lord. I hadn't noticed."

"Will you manage?" he asked abruptly. "You know my views well enough."

"I shall manage," she said with equal abruptness. "I'll bid you good day now, my lord – ma'am."

She turned on her heel and put an arm around the boy's shoulder with rough affection to draw him away. His eyes had never left Felicity's face throughout the conversation and he moved off with reluctance. The other children had long since vanished.

Felicity and Stayne were alone.

"Well, Miss Vale – shall we return home?"

Felicity dragged her gaze away from the retreating figures.

"Is that woman a widow, my lord?"

Something in her voice made the Earl regard her curiously. "Ester Graham? Yes. Her husband was killed in an accident on the estate about six months ago."

"That must have been soon after the baby was born?"

"Yes. She's had a pretty bad time."

"How unfortunate!"

Stayne frowned, but said nothing. He threw her into the saddle and felt the anger in her. When they had ridden for some distance, still in silence, he turned a sideways glance upon her rigid figure.

"Miss Vale," he said mildly, "I have the oddest notion that I have in some way incurred your displeasure – yet I am at a loss to know how."

Felicity had striven very hard to contain her wrath; the back of her neck prickled with the effort. "If you do not know, my lord," she said stiffly, "if your conscience is not stirred, then it is hardly for me to criticize. I will not be brought to book again for not guarding my tongue!"

The Earl was torn between amusement and exasperation. "Oh, for God's sake, girl – out with it! You are quite plainly choking on some grievance, imagined or otherwise."

"I did not imagine that poor woman's plight, my lord – nor can I imagine why she must needs repair her own property when you so obviously maintain all the rest in excellent order."

"Ah – I see! Perhaps, my dear Miss Vale, it is because I do not own Mrs. Graham's cottage. It is her own property."

"Oh!" Felicity was momentarily disconcerted. "But... even so, surely it would not... hurt you... to repair it for her."

"No, madam, it would not," he replied curtly, "but try, if you can, to make her accept my offer. She is as deuced independent as you are yourself." She flushed. "I pay her a small pension – not enough, for I valued Tom Graham highly – he was our head forester as was his father before him. But it is all she will take. Apart from that, we buy our eggs from her and give her all the sewing work from Cheynings."

"And can she manage on that?"

"Barely, I should think, but I can do no more. She could sell the house, of course, and take a living-in post, but she won't. It was given to Tom's father by my father, and it means more to her than a mere roof over her head."

Felicity knew exactly how she must feel – how she would feel herself.

"I believe Captain Hardman made her an offer for it which she turned down very smartly."

"Captain Hardman?"

"Our new neighbor at Manor Court. An unknown quantity as yet," mused the Earl. "I'm told he acquired the Court in lieu of a gambling debt and is already in - creasing the rents of some of his tenant farms to the point where they cannot be met, which does not endear him to me."

"No – indeed!"

"By the way, Miss Vale," Stayne smiled slightly. "I must commend your handling of those young brats ... forceful, but effective."

Felicity's eye flashed with sudden anger. "I abhor persecution of any kind. Have the children no school?"

"I believe there was one in my mother's day, though it was primarily concerned with their souls. The schoolroom is still there alongside the church, but it has long since fallen into disuse and I doubt our present incumbent would be keen to revive it."

"Well, that is a pity. Apart from the many greater benefits, it would keep the children out of mischief."

The Earl looked faintly amused. "A strange remark coming from someone who has had anything but an ordered upbringing. Are you then in favor of education for the masses, Miss Vale?"

"Yes," she answered without hesitation. "Perhaps because of my upbringing. I have seen a great deal of downright misery in my travels. Poor people put upon by everyone – by their governments, by the armies of both sides

– and submitting because they were too ignorant to assert themselves.

"And pray, do not seek to tell me, my lord, as I am so often told, that the poor are happy in their lot – it puts me out of all patience!"

The Earl drew back on his rein and stopped. "Good God!" he exclaimed in mock horror. "Don't tell me I have been harboring a Radical under my roof all these weeks!"

His reaction prompted an unwilling trill of laughter, but Felicity's eyes remained serious. "Perhaps I am. At any rate, it is a subject upon which I feel most strongly."

"Palpably so. And you think my estate brats should be given the advantages of a good education, do you, Miss Vale? So that they may later turn and murder me in my bed?"

"I do not consider that in the least likely, sir," she said primly. "I would judge you to be a just employer and landlord."

"You overwhelm me, ma'am!"

"But there are many, like your Captain Hardman, who are not," she persisted. "I have been long enough in England to sense the unrest – and know that it is growing. Surely, in the long term, it is better that people should be well taught, so that they may gain their objectives by reasoned argument, rather than by violence?"

"H'm!" The Earl gave her one of his long-nosed stares. Then he turned and set his horse in motion again.

"Very well, ma'am – I am open to conviction." There was a touch of malice in the harsh voice. "As from now, you are appointed to the post of schoolmistress here."

Felicity's first reaction to the Earl's pronouncement was that he had taken temporary leave of his senses, the second was a fervent wish that she had kept her mouth shut. She hastily assembled a string of arguments intended to persuade him that she was quite unequal to such a task.

He demolished them all. "Don't underestimate your ability to handle children, Miss Vale. You have already wrought wonders with Jamie."

Felicity looked at him closely, but could discern no trace of levity. In desperation she urged, "But what about Jamie?"

"Oh, Jamie will do well enough," he said crisply. "We will engage some suitable young woman to play the nursemaid until Mr. Burnett arrives. And you may give him an hour or so's tuition each day at some period best suited to yourself."

She was fast adapting herself to the Earl's odd, abrupt ways, yet this calm assumption that all was decided roused conflicting emotions. She longed to give him a sharp set-down, but was lured by the challenge of starting a school.

"Very well, my lord. I am willing to consider your proposition. What salary are you offering?"

Steyne looked taken aback. "I have no idea, Miss Vale. What is the current stipend for schoolteachers, I wonder? How

94

does forty pounds per annum sound to you?"

It sounded like music. "Make it forty-five, sir – and I will accept."

"O – ho! So we are to haggle, are we? I seem to remember, not many days since, you were all for throwing my money back at me!"

"That was quite different," Felicity maintained. "More in the nature of a favor for a favor. This is business."

He gave a short bark of laughter. "A woman of principle, egad! Well, madam – I shall not haggle with you. You shall have your forty-five pounds, but I warn you that in return I shall demand nothing short of excellence!"

Chapter Five

The schoolhouse was in a sad state of dilapidation. It stood back from the lane, screened from the church by a small coppice. Felicity viewed it with Mr. Becket, his lordship's agent, and together they decided how to make it not only habitable, but also cheerful to work in. Mr. Becket's instructions were to equip it exactly to Miss Vale's requirements.

A gig, together with a delightfully mannered black gelding, had been put at her disposal, and there was a tacit understanding that she might also ride Starlight whenever she wished, but a tentative proposal that she should take up residence in the diminutive dwelling adjoining the schoolroom was firmly rejected.

"No, Miss Vale," said the Earl.

"Under no circumstances will I entertain such a notion. You will continue to live at Cheynings. Not only is the schoolhouse totally unsuited to a young girl living alone . . ."

"You flatter me, my lord," she put in, amused. "I am two and twenty, you know – and have been out of leading strings for years. I am well able to take care of myself."

"I do not doubt it, ma'am. I cannot imagine you were ever easy to lead, but my decision remains unaltered. Putting other considerations aside, there is Jamie. Would you desert him?"

Of course she would not – and so all her hastily assembled arguments were quashed before they ever found utterance.

A nursemaid had been found locally for Jamie – a sensible country girl who had grown up in a large family and knew exactly how a small boy's mind worked. Amaryllis was not overly pleased by Rose Hibberd's appointment, but this was due mostly to a perverse resentment of Felicity's new-found independence.

Miss Vale and her gig were soon a familiar sight in the village. News of the proposed school had traveled fast, and if the children were unsure, their parents were not. Offers of help flooded in, but it was Ester Graham who haunted the schoolroom, drawn there from the very first; it was Ester who helped to lay out benches and to unpack the shiny new slates, while young Willie stood staring at Felicity, unblinking and expressionless, and the baby crooned in a basket nearby.

Felicity had been unsure how many the school was to cater for and in the end she had been obliged to consult Lord Stayne.

"I am in some difficulty, my lord," she began. "Do you wish me to take only the children of your own workers and tenants, or is the school to be open to all?"

"I have given the matter very little thought, Miss Vale. Is it important?"

"Well, sir, I have been approached by

several people . . ."

"From the Manor Court estate?"

"Yes," said Felicity. "They seem very keen."

"Then you must do as you think best," said the Earl with patent disinterest. "I would not hazard a guess as to Hardman's views. He is away at present, I believe. He has iron foundries in Shropshire which take a great deal of his time. I doubt he will concern himself overmuch. Yes. Do as you please in the matter."

Felicity took a deep breath. "Then . . . may I make a suggestion, sir?"

He viewed her with deep misgivings. "I have the oddest conviction that I am about to be cozened."

"Nothing of the kind, my lord." She met his bright dark gaze with equanimity. "I wanted to ask you about Ester Graham."

"What about Ester Graham?"

"Would you consider employing her as my assistant at the school? She is well educated and if we are to have greater numbers I should find her help invaluable."

The bright gaze never wavered and his continuing silence made her jumpy. Her words tumbled out in a rush. "Well, you did make a point of telling me that you would help her more if you could!"

The Earl sat on a corner of his desk and folded his arms. "So I did, Miss Vale. You have an excellent memory. I do trust you are not going to store up all my little bon mots and trot them out when occasion demands. I should not know a moment's ease!" He scowled. "How much is it to be this time?"

"I beg your pardon, sir?"

"How much am I to pay Mrs. Graham? Come now – do you not wish to negotiate her salary? You drove a hard enough bargain with regard to your own. Surely she is worthy of equal resolution?"

Felicity turned bright crimson and was almost provoked into indiscretion; but she must not jeopardize Ester's chances, so she strove to compose a calm reply.

The Earl continued to observe her. "You are slow to answer, Miss Vale. Shall I tell you how you appear, sitting there in your neat black gown with your eyes cast down and your hands clasped demurely in your lap? You are the very picture of a submissive young woman."

He brought his hand down on the desk with a suddenness that made her jump, and came to his feet. "But you are a sham, madam!" He stood before her and took her chin between finger and thumb. "There is no trace of submissiveness in you – not in this chin, which can set itself so stubbornly against me – nor yet in your eyes. Ah! There – you see? It is your eyes that are your undoing every time! They fizz and smolder with yellow flames the moment your temper is tested – as now!"

"Then why must you provoke it?" she protested, her chin still firmly imprisoned in his clasp.

"I have no idea, Miss Vale. Mayhap I

see your persistent refusal to be cowed as an irresistible challenge." His fierce glance, now frowning, swept over her. "Why do you wear your hair in that ugly knot?"

Felicity found this sudden shift disconcerting. She said breathlessly, "It seemed ... appropriate to my circumstances, sir."

"It may well be the accepted mode for aspiring governesses and schoolmarms, but I cannot think it necessary in your case – and it don't become you."

The Earl released her abruptly and walked to the window, leaving Felicity to wonder if she would ever wholly understand him. Yet she found herself smiling as she stood up.

"I confess I should be very glad to change it, my lord," she said – and hesitated. "About Ester Graham, sir?"

"Ah yes – Ester Graham." He swung around. "Well, my tenacious young friend – what am I to pay your proposed assistant?"

"I believe thirty pounds per annum

would be fair," Felicity said firmly.

"Do you now? And you are doubtless of the opinion that I can well afford such a sum!" She thought she detected a gleam in his eye. "So be it. You have your assistant."

"Thank you, sir. Ester will be overjoyed."

As she turned to leave he added dryly, "You are not likely to increase your staff still further, I trust? Should you find any more lame ducks, I feel bound to warn you that I am by no means the soft touch you seem to think me."

Ester refused to take the news of her appointment seriously and needed to be convinced that it was not charity. Once satisfied, however, her face lost much of its haggard look; there was a new lightness in her step and she began to look much nearer to her twenty-seven years. She had security within her grasp – something she had not thought possible.

And so have I, thought Felicity, as she brushed out the despised knot for the

103

last time. Lord Stayne might be exasperating, infuriating even, and at times downright overbearing, but that she could cope with. It was infinitely preferable to the dreaded prospect of some Mrs. Lipscombe-like dragon to whom one would have to be pleasant for fear of losing one's place.

She gazed pensively at her reflection and wondered whether his lordship ever saw Lucinda Lipscombe in the guise of a challenge. Surely not, for she would have been schooled to show only the most biddable and pleasing side of her nature in the presence of so eligible a prospect. I bet she sulks like the very devil when she is crossed, Felicity decided uncharitably.

The school was going to be a resounding success. Felicity was sure by the end of the first week. She had nineteen boys and fifteen girls ranging from seven to twelve – a variation in both age and capabilities which challenged her resources to the utmost. In spite of their initial reluctance, all but a few were quickly won over by Felicity's cheerful, matter-of-fact approach.

She was well aware that the Earl was watching her progress with an uncomfortable degree of interest – he had several times dropped in on them quite without warning, thus putting her on her mettle.

It was particularly galling when he arrived a few weeks before Christmas accompanied by Miss Lipscombe, in a riding dress of ruby velvet, to find Felicity sitting on the top of her desk amid a circle of upturned faces, with her guitar on her knee, singing a Spanish carol to which the children had learned a simple chorus.

Felicity was not aware of their presence until Ester touched her arm. She slid to her feet in confusion; the well-drilled children bobbed their greeting and were sent back to their laborious copying.

She intercepted a glance of disapproval tinged with incredulity directed by Miss Lipscombe at Lord Stayne which roused her to meet the Earl's high-nosed stare with a measure of defiance.

"The children have worked so hard this morning, I decided they were in need of a little relaxation. We are practicing very hard for a Christmas concert."

His expression remained unfathomable.

Lucinda Lipscombe, however, was more forthcoming. "Surely, Miss Vale," she said with an air of sweet reasonableness, "if the children are to be taught singing at all, which I am sure my mamma would not hold to be necessary, a simple English song would be preferable – and more instructive. To be teaching them a foreign language before they have mastered their own hardly makes good sense."

"I cannot agree, ma'am," Felicity's voice was cool, though anger raged within her. "They pick up the Spanish with surprising ease, and I hold that anything which inspires their confidence and encourages them to express them-

106

selves at this stage is invaluable."

"Then we must hope that your ... experiments ... succeed, Miss Vale. It would not do for you to be abusing the trust Lord Stayne has placed in you."

The arch look which accompanied this honeyed reproof was wasted on his lordship, who had been casually perusing the children's work. He looked up with a derisive smile.

"Your methods, if unorthodox, appear to achieve results, Miss Vale. There is a distinct improvement since my last visit."

"Thank you, my lord." The victory was a small one, but sweet – and Lucinda's discomposure sufficient reward. It was as well to bask in his approval while she may; it was inevitable that sooner or later she would fall foul of it.

Rose Hibberd had been confined to her bed with a cold and Jamie, with only old Nurse to watch him, was making the most of his chances. Several times Felicity had discovered him tucked away at the back of her classroom, ineffectively concealed by the rest of the children. She entirely sympathized with his yearning for young company – and thought it no bad thing for him to be mixing with those less fortunate than himself – yet she could not suppose that either his mother or the Earl would share her views.

Even less would they have appreciated his ripening friendship with Lanny Price; of all the soulmates to have chosen, Lanny was the most potentially disastrous to a boy of Jamie's questing spirit. Red-haired and incredibly slight for all his nine years, Lanny was the son of the most slippery poacher in the area, and was already set to rival his father's reputation.

Felicity did all in her power to discourage the unholy alliance; beyond this, she could only pray that it would die of natural causes. Her prayers were destined to go unheeded.

One morning the schoolroom door

crashed back to admit Lord Stayne – his greatcoat flapping, his face like thunder. With a sinking heart Felicity saw that he was not alone; two small, grimacing boys, each held inexorably by the ear, were frog-marched up to her desk.

"Miss Vale," he snapped without preamble, "I would be obliged if you will make clear to your brats that my woods are out of bounds."

Felicity flushed, but said calmly, "They have already been so instructed, my lord."

"Have they!" He thrust the wriggling Lanny forward. "Then how is it, do you suppose, that I find this young whelp wreaking havoc in my covers, making my birds as crazed as be-damned?"

"I have no idea, sir."

"And I suppose you have no idea how my nephew comes to be in his company, either – or do you perhaps consider it necessary to Jamie's education that he should be initiated into the art of poaching my pheasants?"

Felicity, stung by the cutting sarcasm

109

and plagued by guilt, flung the two boys a look of burning reproach. Jamie had the grace to hang his head, but Lanny stood four square, red hair on end, bristling with defiance and injured pride.

"We wasn't poachin'. Fat chance I'd have to lift so much as a dozy old hen with him threshin' about!" His head jerked toward Jamie; the accompanying sniff was loaded with contempt.

There was a smothered giggle from the classroom. Felicity's own lips twitched, but the Earl showed no such weakness, so she said with unaccustomed sharpness, "Be silent, children. Get on with your work. Lanny, I am ashamed of you, of both of you – during school hours, too! You will apologize at once to his lordship for the trouble you have caused. At once, Lanny."

The apologies were grudgingly offered and grimly received.

"Well, I suppose that must suffice," she said dryly. "As for punishment . . ." She looked hopefully at the Earl, who

110

was not in the least disposed to be lenient.

"I shall deal with Jamie," he said tersely. "This young pup I leave to you. I trust you will make a sufficient impression upon him to discourage any further forays into my covers."

Felicity didn't enjoy administering corporal punishment; a lifetime with the regiment had not convinced her that the barbaric floggings, so much a part of army discipline, achieved anything but pain and misery and, in the end, brutalization.

Until now she had managed to keep order without recourse to the strap, so it was hard to say who suffered most in what followed. Lanny Price took his chastisement with a kind of fierce stoicism and apparently bore her no grudge – but Felicity's hands were shaking as she laid the strap back on the cupboard shelf and locked the door.

Ester, who had offered to relieve her of the unpleasant task, gave her a searching look, but encountered an overbright eye which dared her to comment.

For the first time, Felicity was glad to close the school door behind her. It was not yet dark, but the November sky was dreary, in keeping with her mood. The gig was already pointing homeward when she heard the cry; it was piercing, scarcely human. She reined in and even as she waited, uncertain, it came again, setting her teeth on edge and her back hairs pricking.

She almost fled in a panic, but such an action seemed both cowardly and churlish. Something – or someone was in the most dreadful agony; perhaps an animal caught in a trap. It was coming from Captain Hardman's land. That did give her pause. A notice on the chained-up gate stated the penalties for trespass and from all she had heard, they would be exacted without compunction.

Unable any longer to shut her ears to the cry for help, she jumped from the gig and tied the rein securely to an overhanging branch. She was obliged to hitch up her skirt in order to climb the gate, and found what she was seeking in a clearing not far into the trees.

A small brindled dog had been tied to a tree and a boy was thrashing it unmercifully. Felicity wrenched the whip from his hand before he was aware of her presence.

"How dare you! Give me back my property this instant!" The boy was not above ten years – a stiff-legged embodiment of rage and pomposity. "You are trespassing on my father's land. You will be very sorry when he finds out!"

"And you will be very sorry if I turn this ... weapon upon you as you deserve," returned Felicity angrily. "Does your father know that you use it to ill-treat helpless creatures?"

"Of course he does. My father says it is the only way to exact obedience from one's inferiors – whether they be men or animals."

Felicity was silenced. She wondered what kind of a monster would foster such an appalling philosophy in his own son. She was not long finding out.

"Geoffrey! What goes on here?"

Felicity swung around – and stared. If there had been time to form some picture in her mind of the boy's father, she would have been sadly out. Captain Hardman was short in stature; his stirrup leathers had been taken up to a point that made his feet stick out ludicrously from the horse's belly and he had the kind of figure which defied all the attempts of his tailor to pass him off as a gentleman. Felicity had the illusion that it must be the tightness of his cravat which accounted for his unhealthy pallor – and caused the pale blue eyes to bulge.

But it was the voice which surprised her most – an overlight voice for a man – stilted, expressionless, and unaccountably chilling.

"You are trespassing, madam."

The boy shot a look of smug malevolence. "Yes, Father – she is – she is! And she has taken away my whip. Make her give it back!"

The pale eyes unhurriedly assessed the

scene and came finally to rest on Felicity. She repressed an involuntary desire to shiver.

"Well, madam?"

"I had little choice, sir. Your son was beating this poor wretched animal until its screams could be heard from the road. I came to investigate."

"You are new here, I think. Your name?"

"Vale, sir. Miss Felicity Vale."

Something flickered for a moment in his eyes and was gone. The boy gazed at her with renewed interest.

"She's the schoolmarm, Father! The one you said . . ."

"Be silent, Geoffrey." There was no raising of the voice – no noticeable change of emphasis – yet the boy shrank a little. "Go back to the house and take that . . . creature with you. Give it to Masterson to treat or we shall have the flies feeding off its sores."

His callous indifference infuriated Felicity.

"I was only doing what you said," the

boy muttered. "Titus refused to come to heel – and I punished him."

"I will hear your explanations later. Do as you are bid or Titus will not be alone in his punishment."

The boy untied the dog and slunk away, dragging it, whimpering, at his heels.

The Captain waited until all sound had died away.

"Come here!"

Felicity bristled. "Certainly not. I have nothing to say to you, save that I deplore your callousness and its inevitable consequences upon your son. I bid you good day."

She swept around on her heel, but the thin voice came again.

"You are on my land, madam – and will remain until I give you leave to go. Furthermore, I want none of your highty-tighty schoolroom airs. Now, come here."

It was hard to explain why she complied. She told herself it would be politic to humor him, but that reasoning took

116

no account of the trembling in her legs.

Captain Hardman still held his son's whip. He leaned forward, allowing the lash to brush Felicity's cheek. She set her teeth and glared up at him, meeting a contemptuous, flicking appraisal which was reflected in his next words.

"I should not have thought you a stupid woman, Miss Vale – yet you seem bent upon behaving foolishly in all manner of directions. That Graham woman, for instance. Your friendship with her can do you nothing but harm. Pray – do not interrupt!" he snapped with sudden venom as she opened her mouth to protest.

"And then we come to this school of yours. It does not please me, madam; had I not been away on business it would not have gone thus far unchallenged. If you are wise, you will abandon the project and return whence you came."

Indignation was coursing through Felicity's blood, sweeping caution aside. "You are not only insolent, Captain, you are also ill-informed! The school 'project,' as you term it, is not mine to abandon. You must address yourself to Lord Stayne."

The whip jerked just sufficiently to flick her cheek. "Oh, I shall do so, madam – I mean to make it plain that there will be no foolish notions fostered amongst my workers here. The more ignorant they remain, the better it will suit me, for let me tell you there is nothing like a little learning for breeding sedition – and sedition breeds riots, as I know from my foundries."

"Then I am sorry for you," said Felicity quietly. "But I am even sorrier for the children concerned, since you obviously mean to withdraw them from the school."

"And do you think that will suffice, Miss Vale? Do you imagine that my people will not envy those in the village with greater advantages and seek some means of redressing the balance?"

"The matter is between you and Lord Stayne. There is nothing I can do."

"I do not agree. What does Stayne pay you?"

"I beg your pardon?"

He moved impatiently. "Everything has a price, madam. What is the price of a schoolmarm? No matter. Whatever it is, I will pay more. You can come to Manor Court to try and see if you can instill some knowledge into my Geoffrey. His present tutor is no damned use."

Felicity could not disguise her instant revulsion. "Thank you, Captain Hardman," she said tersely. "But I have no wish to teach your son. I am well satisfied with my present position."

His eyes narrowed to pin points. "Then we must pray you do not regret your decision, madam."

The whip flicked for a third time, and this time the sting of it made her smart. Her anger rose. She seized the trailing lash and held it at arm's length.

"I will not regret anything, Captain. And now I really must beg you to excuse me. Do not seek to detain me, for I am already late – and have left my gig at your gate where it may readily be seen by anyone coming to look for me."

For a moment their glances locked; then he jerked the whip petulantly from her grasp, wheeled his horse, and thundered off into the trees, leaving Felicity limp and more shaken than she cared to admit.

The leaden sky was shedding its first spots of rain; by the time she reached Cheynings it had become a steady downpour. She ran from the stables to the house, longing only for the privacy of her room where she might compose her frayed nerves, but the sound of raised voices reached her before she had gained the first landing. Cavanah came from the small drawing room and for the first time Felicity saw him at a loss. His troubled face cleared hopefully on seeing her.

"Miss Vale! Thank goodness you are come! Have you seen young Master Jamie? He is nowhere to be found and Madam is distracted!"

The petty tyrannies of the day were

swept from Felicity's mind; she closed the drawing-room door and stood with her back against it taking in the scene. Amaryllis lay prone upon a sofa in the throes of near-hysteria, with Rose Hibberd close by, red-eyed and far from well, twisting her fingers in a quite untypical gesture of nerves.

Before the fireplace stood Lord Stayne. Felicity saw that his patience was stretched to the breaking point. She judged that calm was the first priority if anything was to be achieved.

"Cavanah tells me Jamie is missing," she said lightly. "What a monstrous disagreeable boy he is, to be sure – putting everyone about in such a fashion!"

All eyes were on her. In the Earl's she thought she detected a glimmer of relief.

"Thank God!" he said tersely. "Here is someone, at least, who does not treat a child's prank as though it were a Greek tragedy!"

"Maxim! How can you be so unfeeling! Jamie has been gone three hours!" sobbed Amaryllis, her delightful lower

lip quivering with the force of her emotions. Felicity thought inconsequentially
that few people had crying down to such
a fine art as Amaryllis. Even though her
grief was quite genuine, she cried so . . .
becomingly! One could not fail to be
sympathetic. She put a comforting arm
around her cousin's shoulders.

"Then he will be confoundedly bored
by now and wishing to be found. You
may depend upon it, my dear."

Amaryllis shook her off. "You don't
understand. The poor darling was terrified! And I'm sure I don't wonder at it!"

Felicity straightened up, puzzled, and
sought Stayne's reassurance.

"Fustian!" he exclaimed irritably.
"Jamie was instructed to present himself in the library and he cried off. He will
be lying doggo somewhere, seeking to
evade retribution!"

Felicity had quite forgotten the morning's events and their consequences. "Oh
dear, poor Jamie!"

"You may well say so!" Amaryllis
cried passionately. "He would never

have known that horrid boy, but for you!"

The truth of this accusation filled Felicity with guilt. "Then it is up to me to find him."

"He isn't in the house, miss," said Rose fearfully. "We've turned it upside down."

"No. But I believe I know where he is." She looked out at the rain and the darkening sky. "And if I don't fetch him directly, he will get a well-deserved soaking."

When she was halfway across the lawns the heavens opened anew. She put her head down, picked up her skirts, and ran. At the lakeside she turned aside to peer into a thicket of trees, now mostly bare of leaf. There was the shape of something dark – the remains of a tree house. She shouted.

There was a rustling above, and a slithering – and a very small, very bedraggled boy landed with a sodden thud at her feet.

Felicity looked into the scared face

and found time to give him a quick hug before grabbing his hand.

"Come along, my lad. Show me how fast you can run."

"I didn't mean to stay so long," Jamie sobbed as they ran. "But Uncle Max was very angry . . ."

"Well, of course he was angry, stoopid. You behaved very badly, both of you. But Lanny has taken his punishment without complaint."

"Oh!" There was a hiccuped sob. "I 'spect Uncle Max will be more angrier than ever now . . . I only meant to hide until you came. I waited and waited . . ."

Felicity's heart smote her. She had neglected him of late. Poor lamb! His hair was plastered to his head and rain ran down his face to mingle with his tears. She put a protective arm around him, urging him on as he stumbled.

A figure loomed ahead of them. It was the Earl carrying an enormous umbrella. Without a word he scooped Jamie up under one arm and, signaling

Felicity to keep close, they ran for the house.

Amaryllis came running down the staircase as they reached the hall, Rose Hibberd in her wake. She exclaimed at the sight of her son standing in a growing pool of water with a decided hangdog air.

"Rose – take Jamie upstairs at once! He must be got out of those wet clothes if we are to escape a severe inflammation of the lungs!"

"One moment, if you please!" The Earl spoke sharply. "Jamie, when you are dry you will come to the library."

Jamie looked apprehensive; his mother flew at once to his defense.

"Maxim! You would not . . . Jamie has suffered enough. He must go straight to his bed!"

"Nonsense, Amaryllis! A good rubdown and a change of clothes should suffice. Don't pamper the child – you do him a disservice." He met Jamie's shifting gaze. "Shall we say one hour, Jamie?"

The boy nodded reluctantly. Before Amaryllis could open her mouth again, Felicity intervened to suggest that Rose did not look at all well and that, as Jamie's mamma, she must surely wish to supervise Jamie's toilet for herself. A further gentle reminder that he should not be kept standing about in his wet clothes sent the whole party upstairs without delay.

In the silence that followed, the Earl surveyed his schoolmistress and said with surprising mildness, "Thank you. I see you are able to organize others to an inch . . . but should you not change out of your own wet clothes? We do not want you taking a chill."

She put a hand to the hair which had come down and now hung around her shoulders in dripping tendrils.

"Not I," she laughed.

"Ah no – I was forgetting. You are a seasoned campaigner, are you not?"

The gentle irony brought confusion and she moved away. At the stairs she turned. "My lord?"

At once his face hardened. "I hope you will not plead Jamie's cause?"

"No. He has behaved badly and must, of course, be punished. But I do feel some degree of responsibility; if you could just take into account that he is but a small boy who has never been much subjected to discipline until lately?"

The Earl's face was unreadable. "I am not a monster, Miss Vale."

"No, sir – of course not." She half smiled and left him.

It crossed her mind as she stripped off her wet clothes that she should have told him about Captain Hardman, but the thought of another confrontation in a day already fraught with problems was too much to contemplate. Her head was throbbing; all she really wished to do was to lie down, but the memory of Amaryllis's distress plagued her.

Her cousin was prostrate upon her bed when Felicity sought her out. Curtains of heavy gold brocade were drawn across the windows and a single lamp was shaded so that it did not shine in her eyes.

"Dorcas tells me you have the migraines," Felicity murmured sympathetically. "How horrid for you."

Amaryllis turned a fretful, tear-drenched face on the pillow. "Nobody cares how I suffer! Maxim accounts it mere self-indulgence!"

"Oh, but then, men are quite insensitive to all disorders – except their own! I know how utterly wretched migraine can make one feel, for Mrs. Patterson suffered most dreadfully from time to time. There is a special tisane I used to infuse for her. Perhaps it would relieve you?"

"You are so . . . strong!" Amaryllis sighed, when she was presently persuaded to sit forward and sip the soothing potion. "I daresay you will think me a very poor creature, only I cannot help it if my nerves are delicate."

"No, indeed," Felicity reassured her, wishing very much that she, too, might comfortably succumb to a strong attack of nerves. "But you must not fret about

Jamie, you know. The discipline will do him no harm."

Amaryllis shuddered. "He should not have been chastised."

"Well, he has borne it with disgusting cheerfulness. I have just heard him bragging to all who will listen that Lord Stayne had called him 'a plucky young 'un' and was to take him fishing next week."

"I hate this place! I had such a pretty house in Chelsea – and so many friends, but Maxim was adamant that it was quite the wrong place to bring up Jamie. He never cared a jot when Antony was alive! I wish he would marry and produce a whole brood of heirs – and then I could go back to Chelsea and be happy."

She met Felicity's eye and moved uncomfortably, the ready tears starting again. "You think me very foolish and unfeeling, don't you? Perhaps I am. I suppose I loved Antony . . . he was very gay and charming, not in the least like his brother . . . but he was so seldom home and one cannot grieve forever!

And then there was Mamma . . . it is very disagreeable to have been in mourning for so long . . ." She broke off abruptly, aware that even for her, she had been appallingly tactless. "Oh, I am sorry!"

"Don't be," Felicity said briskly, standing up.

"I . . . I haven't been very nice to you, have I?" ventured Amaryllis. "You must have been very unhappy."

"Well, if I was, I am not any longer . . . and perhaps we shall be better friends in the future."

"Yes, I should like that," said Amaryllis slowly. "You are a very . . . comfortable person to be with. Did you never wish to marry?"

"I never found anyone I liked well enough." Felicity grinned. "Or perhaps they didn't like me! Men do so like us to be fragile, and it is not easy to feign helplessness when one is obviously built to hold one's own . . . as your Mr. Dytton found to his cost!"

Amaryllis flushed at the reminder, her lower lip caught artlessly between small white teeth. "You are certainly never at a loss. You manage Maxim so well. Do you not find him overbearing?"

"At times!" Felicity admitted with feeling. "But then, I have always been used to men who bark orders, so I have very little sensibility!"

Chapter Six

Something was worrying Ester; she jumped on the children for the slightest mistake – and when she had snapped at Willie for the second time, Felicity determined to speak.

Ester hedged at first, and then brought out the letter. It was from Captain Hardman – a renewal of his offer to buy the cottage, politely worded, yet it made Felicity's scalp prickle.

"Show it to Lord Stayne," she advised bluntly.

"Why? Because he is a magistrate? There's no need. I have no intention of selling."

"Is Lord Stayne a magistrate?" exclaimed Felicity, diverted. "All the better then. He'll be able to judge it with an expert eye."

"I tell you, there's no need. There was

never less need for me to sell. With this job I am now secure."

"I still don't like it. I can't put my finger on it, but there is a threat in that letter somewhere."

Ester wavered.

"Lord Stayne would know," Felicity persisted. "He would be able to advise you."

"I don't need advice. I can manage my own affairs."

"Then why have you been snapping everyone's head off this morning? You're worried, Ester. I've met the Captain, remember."

"From what you told me, I doubt he will easily forget the encounter," said Ester dryly.

The Earl said much the same thing. After Hardman's protest visit, he had castigated her for not informing him of her meeting with the Captain.

"It ... slipped my mind, sir," she had lied meekly.

"Hm – Strange! It did not slip Captain Hardman's mind. Indeed, one might suppose it to have been seared upon his memory!" He gave her a hard look. "If you wish your school to continue, you would be well advised not to make an enemy of Hardman. He is a dangerous man."

Her chin rose a fraction. "I will remember, my lord. But I will not be threatened – or coerced!"

"Nor will you again trespass on private land, if you please."

The Manor Court children were withdrawn, to everyone's regret, and as far as Felicity was concerned that was the end of the matter – until about ten days before Christmas, when the schoolhouse was broken into and wrecked.

She arrived to find every bench, every slate smashed, and whitewash splashed over everything. The children were sent home and in growing anger she and Ester set about clearing up the mess. They were soon overwhelmed with helpers, and by the time the Earl arrived on the scene most of the room had been cleared, the mangled contents tossed outside to await burning, and the floor scrubbed clean.

Grim-faced, he took stock of the situation, and Felicity felt her antagonism rising. The elegance of his mulberry driving coat made her feel dusty and disheveled.

"Pray do not scruple to say what I am sure you are itching to say, my lord!"

"What is that, Miss Vale?"

"Why, that I should not have crossed Captain Hardman – that my unbridled tongue is responsible for this ... outrage."

"Is that what you believe?"

She shrugged. "Oh, I know some of the women think the Manor Court children responsible, but children cannot destroy solid wooden desks so systematically." Tears of anger threatened, but were blinked away. "So much waste! All because of one man's pique."

"I think this goes deeper than mere pique, Miss Vale."

Felicity followed him into the now-empty room where some of the village women still mopped and scrubbed. "I begin to wonder if this whole venture was not hastily conceived," he murmured, half to himself.

"No!" She protested. "You surely do not mean to be so easily routed?"

The Earl's brows rose haughtily. "My dear Miss Vale, I was not aware that we were conducting a military campaign."

"No, sir . . . of course not. But you wouldn't . . . you couldn't contemplate closing the school?"

"Something tells me I am not to be permitted to do so," he drawled. "Doubtless I shall be expected to refit this emporium of learning, and take steps to guard it against further assault!"

"Oh, as to the latter, sir, we need not trouble you," said Felicity briskly. "I have mustered a sufficient number of the children's parents to mount permanent dusk-to-dawn pickets."

"Have you, be damn!" exclaimed his lordship.

"Yes, sir. The men have been most cooperative. I think I can promise there will be no repeat of last night's trouble."

"Then I suppose you must have your refit." The Earl swung on his heel and Felicity followed him outside. He turned to rake her with a glance. "Come. I will drive you home. You look tired."

"No – really!" she said, flustered. "I ... thank you, sir, but I must stay to see everything completed."

"Why? Is Ester Graham not competent to supervise the remainder?"

"Yes, but ..."

"Well then." He stepped back to the doorway. "Ester, I am taking Miss Vale home. We may safely leave all here in your charge, may we not?"

"Certainly, my lord," Ester said mildly, noting her friend's ruffled manner. "A very good idea. She has worked herself to a standstill."

"Why – so I thought. You see, Miss Vale – there is no problem."

Felicity disliked the way she was being maneuvered. "You forget, my lord," she said crisply, "I have my own conveyance."

"I had not forgot. Percy shall drive the gig. I am sure such a task is not beyond him, is it, child?"

The young tiger was uncertain whether this was to be taken as a compliment or no, but the prospect of tooling even a single horse and gig the length of the carriageway persuaded him not to probe the Earl's words for hidden insults.

There was no more to be said. Felicity's pelisse was fetched. She suffered the Earl to slip it over her shoulders and hand her up into his curricle, a brand-new acquisition with huge, brilliant yellow wheels. For all of a hundred yards she maintained an injured silence, but the horsewoman in her was soon surreptitiously observing the Earl, noting with reluctant admiration the fine, light hands on the reins, the skill with which he pointed his leaders, the whip's thong flicking out and whistling soundlessly back up the stick, to be caught with a deft flick of the wrist.

Felicity's own fingers twitched with longing; only once had she driven a four in hand, and they had been nothing like such light-mouthed beauties as these! She folded her hands resolutely in her lap and turned her thoughts to the day's events and from thence to Ester. She sighed.

Stayne's glance was enigmatic. "You are understandably cast down, Miss Vale. But take heart; if I am not mistaken, you will have come about by morning."

Her ready smile flickered. "I daresay you are right, sir. As it happens, my sighs were for Ester."

"I thought we had solved Mrs. Graham's problems. What ails her now?"

Felicity explained about the letter.

"A carefully veiled threat?" suggested the Earl.

"That was my immediate reaction. I wanted her to show you the letter, but she would not admit the necessity. After what has happened today, I begin to wonder if we have the beginnings of a campaign of intimidation."

"Your reasons, ma'am?" demanded Stayne.

"That's just it, sir. I'm not sure you would consider them sufficient. But the women were talking today as they worked... it seems that Lanny Price's father..."

Here Felicity faltered, unsure quite how to proceed; uncertain of the ethics of propounding to a magistrate the findings of an undoubted poacher. His lordship helped her out of her difficulty.

"What you are loath to tell me about Dick Price is hardly a secret, Miss Vale. I am well aware that he works for me by day and robs me at night."

"Oh, you know!" she exclaimed, relieved.

"I believe he lives rather better off my game than I do myself," he said dryly. "Though I suspect his family derive little benefit."

"No, indeed. They say he drinks it all. Well, it seems he has been ... frequenting Manor Court estates recently, and he says Hardman has several men – strangers – wandering the grounds."

"That hardly surprises me, Miss Vale. With the shooting season at its peak, it is not unnatural that Captain Hardman should take steps to protect his birds."

"No, sir – except that Price seems ready to swear the men are not game-keepers – not country men at all, in fact. But they are big and rough looking, with one huge Negro among their number. Price reckons they have been brought in from one of Hardman's foundries."

"And to your ever-fertile imagination this suggests an incipient policy of harassment?"

Felicity was indignant. "I did not imagine those smashed desks! And if Ester should be exposed to similar tactics ..."

"What would you have me do about it?" The question was impatient to the point of curtness. "We may suspect all we will, Miss Vale, but I can hardly question the Captain's right to keep

141

whatever labor force he pleases within the confines of his estate. Unless they can be apprehended in the act of violence, my hands are tied!"

"Yes, I do see that, my lord. Does that mean there is no way of protecting Ester?"

The Earl's tone was crisp. "On the contrary, my dear girl, there are several if only she can be brought to lay aside that confounded pride of hers for long enough to consider them."

"Well, I am a touch independent myself, you know," Felicity confided, with sublime understatement. "So I can appreciate her reluctance to accept help. But I am sure you will discover a way to overcome her reticence. You are seldom at a loss."

"You are too generous, ma'am!" The Earl swept the curricle around a tight bend in the drive, displaying an ability to drive to an inch which drew from his companion a swift gasp of admiration.

"Ha! Your opinions are fickle, Miss Vale! There was a time not long since when you took a more jaundiced view of my mastery of the ribbons! You were quite scathingly dogmatic on the subject, as I remember."

Felicity's eyes spilled over into appreciative laughter. "How ungallant in you, my lord, to drag up so mortifying an incident – and with such inaccuracy! Your skill, as I remember, was never in question – only your want of consideration!"

He laughed aloud.

"Beautifully done, Miss Vale! Rolled up, horse, foot, and guns! So. What would you have me do about Ester Graham?"

"I'm not sure. I suppose... you couldn't offer to buy the cottage yourself?"

This drew a mildly incredulous look. "My dear girl, your brain must be addled if you think she would ever agree!"

"No...o," Felicity admitted reluctantly. "She might, of course, if she could be persuaded that it was a temporary measure – part of a scheme to rid the village of Captain Hardman and his henchmen."

"You credit me with too much license, Miss Vale!" said the Earl scathingly. "I am in no position to rid the village of Hardman – would I contemplate such tactics."

"Well, I'm sure I can't see why not. You must agree that everyone would be a great deal more comfortable without him."

There was a note of awe in his voice. "Have you always shown this alarming propensity for organizing people?"

"Only when they will not make a push to help themselves." She grinned and then added on an unintentionally pleading note, "If I can persuade Ester, will you at least see her?"

Stayne sighed. "What can I say, without appearing a monster? Yes – I will see her, Miss Vale. The whole proposition smacks of connivance, but I daresay something may be worked out."

"Thank you, my lord," she said meekly, and gave herself up to the pleasures of the drive. The park was looking particularly fine; the winter sunshine slanted through the bare branches of the elms, giving them an austere, sculptured beauty.

When at last they came in sight of Cheynings they found a post chaise drawn up, its doors thrown open. A portly figure was descending with elaborate, almost mincing care.

He was a truly splendid sight, this aging exquisite; his riding coat, a voluminous affair of many capes and much frogging, was fastened across the chest with a double row of enormous mother-of-pearl buttons. It fell open to reveal a rich silk lining, pale fawn breeches which hugged a still shapely thigh, and gleaming top-boots sporting white turn-down cuffs. All this proclaimed a true Gentleman of the Ton; as though further confirmation were necessary, a fashionable beaver hat was set rakishly atop black locks – suspiciously black for his years, Felicity judged humorously – liberally anointed with Russian oil.

The effect of this apparition upon the Earl was unexpected.

"Oh, good God!" he groaned, "Uncle Peregrine!"

He flung the reins into the hands of a groom and was already several strides away before he recalled Felicity still sitting in the curricle. Impatience darkening his face, he returned and swung her unceremoniously to the ground as though she were featherlight, and left her standing, uncertain whether to go or stay. In the end she stayed to witness the affecting reunion of uncle and nephew.

"Ah, Max, m'boy! There you are then," boomed a jovial voice. "You'll be surprised to see me, no doubt. Fancied a spot of rustication . . . decided to spend a day or two in the bosom of m'family. Knew you'd be glad to see your old uncle, what!"

"Gammon!" returned his lordship with brutal candor. "A repairing lease, more like, if I know you. Creditors breathing down that monstrosity of a neckcloth, are they?"

Felicity thought this a most unfeeling greeting, but it was taken in surprisingly good part, the older gentleman being somewhat preoccupied in supervising the safe bestowal of a great number of boxes and portmanteaus being unloaded under the gimlet eye of a thin, pale man with the neat, dark dress and air of consequence of a gentleman's gentleman.

Their efforts were hampered when a squeal of "Uncle Perry! Uncle Perry!" brought Jamie hurtling down the steps with two yapping spaniels, to fling himself upon the startled exquisite; he was followed only slightly less impetuously by his mother.

Felicity had never seen such a change in anyone; Amaryllis clutched the folds of the magnificent coat with open joy and affection.

"Uncle Perry!" she gasped, laughing. "Why did you not let us know? Oh, I am so glad you are come!"

"Yes, well, have a care do, m'dear!" he pleaded. "And 'ware those buttons, I implore you! Weston assures me they are unique. What a pair you are, to be sure! I shall think myself in Bedlam presently."

But a roguish twinkle belied the rough words and he kissed Amaryllis soundly.

"Egad! This lad of yours has shot up . . . and you prettier than ever, you baggage! But too pale by half." He pinched her cheek. "Tell you what, m'dear . . . comes of being buried down here in this plaguey mausoleum . . . send anyone into a decline!"

He encountered a particularly derisive stare from his nephew – and was fortuitously distracted on the instant. "Fotherby, you blithering idiot! Attend, man! Can you not see how that dolt of a lackey is mangling my bandboxes? That one has my cravats . . . dammit, the fool has it upside down!"

The Earl watched the seemingly unending procession of baggage.

"A few days only I believe you said, Uncle?" he queried with heavy sarcasm.

There was an answering gleam of appreciation in the other's eye. "Why, so I intend. But one must dress, dear boy!"

"Quite," said the Earl. "Well – I must look to my horses. We shall meet at dinner."

Amaryllis tucked her arm under the capacious coat sleeve, and with Jamie hanging on his other side, they drew their much loved relative toward the house.

"Do come along in quickly," she cried. "I am positively dying to hear all the latest on dits. I'll warrant there isn't a breath of scandal has escaped your notice. Oh, how I miss it all!"

For the first time they noticed Felicity, still standing, having enjoyed the whole spectacle hugely. The exquisite paused, his quizzing glass lifted in interested scrutiny.

Jamie ran to drag her forward. "This is Cousin F'licity," he explained with pride.

Felicity was much intrigued by Sir Peregrine Trent. He was brother to the Earl's late mother and as different from his nephew as could be. She met his appreciative glance with amusement.

"Vale? Now where have I . . .? Ah, I have it! Sally . . . Sally Merton . . . ." He turned to Amaryllis. "Your mamma's sister, puss . . . married some soldier laddie against all advice. Quite a kick-up there was! She was all but promised to Hatherford at the time . . . had a bit of an eye to her m'self, come to that! Well, well! So you're Sally Merton's gel? How is your mother, child? Is she here? Egad – I should be delighted to renew our acquaintance!"

"Both my parents are dead." Felicity explained briefly and at once the mask of the dandy dropped; the genuineness of Sir Peregrine's distress was apparent.

"And so you have sought refuge with your little cousin," he said gruffly. "Very proper, m'dear . . . it's what families are for."

"Oh, Felicity is much too independent to be living off her relations!" cried Amaryllis. "She was all set to find some horrid post until Stayne prevailed upon her to open a school in the village."

"That don't sound like Max," Sir Peregrine stated unequivocally. "Always treated his tenants fair and square... not saying otherwise, but a school? Sounds like a hum!"

"Why, so I thought, but sure enough he set it all in motion and now the school is thriving, is it not, Felicity?"

The question brought the angry frustration flooding back, making her account of the day's setback the more vivid.

Amaryllis shuddered. "I knew that man was up to no good. I met him at the Honeysett's some weeks back and thought him a nasty, toad-eating little creature. Why should he want Ester Graham's cottage?"

"Sheer cussedness, I imagine," said Felicity. "Though, from what Lord Stayne has said, he seems to be acquiring land at a disturbing rate."

"Well, Ester's cottage hasn't much land. Perhaps he has an inamorata and wishes to establish her nearby."

"Don't like the sound of the fellow at

all," said Sir Peregrine bluntly. "Regular havey-cavey character, I shouldn't wonder."

He said as much to his nephew later on. The Earl appeared to have recovered from his earlier irritation and after a pleasant family dinner, sat back sipping his port and listening to his uncle rattling on with apparent affability.

"If you'd care for my advice, Max, that one'll bear watching. Might even be prudent to abandon this school nonsense for the present."

A faint quizzical smile touched the Earl's mouth. "Did you suggest as much to Miss Vale?"

His uncle grinned. "Gave me the length of her tongue! Lass of spirit, that one. Tragic – losing both parents at a stroke."

"Yes."

"D'ye know, I might have married her mother . . . well, that may be stretching it a bit, but still . . . what a beauty! You'll remember, no doubt, what a handsome woman Amaryllis's ma was . . . as girls they took the Town by storm. It was the Gunnings all over again. This child must take after the father."

Sir Peregrine took out an intricately worked snuffbox. He flicked it open. "Don't know if you'll care for this. It's a new sort Petersham put up for me."

His lordship declined the honor and said amiably, "Just how deep in dun territory are you this time, Uncle Perry?"

His uncle pocketed the box and dusted his fingers delicately with a large lace handkerchief, pausing to remove an imaginary speck from the glory of his brocade waistcoat.

"You mustn't be troubling yourself about me, Max. I may have been plunging a bit steep, but I shall come about."

"What was it? Pharaoh?"

"Deep basset. It was my weakness. And talking of weaknesses," continued Sir Peregrine with a deft turn of subject, "ain't it time you was thinking of dropping the handkerchief? Not a pleasant thought, I'll grant you, but you owe it to the family, dear boy."

"I'm in no hurry," returned the Earl with surprising mildness. "The succession is secure with Jamie."

"Aye – but is it enough? I mean – God forbid that anything should happen to the lad, but if it did, then everything goes to that damned half-wit, Frampton!" Sir Peregrine shuddered. "Don't bear thinking of . . . the fellow's as wet as a plaguey fish! Heard you was in a fair way to offering for Lipscombe's daughter . . . good connections there, m'boy . . . fine breeding stock, too, and not a bad-looking little filly! Could do worse, if you can stomach the mother."

His nephew's face gave nothing away. "If and when I contemplate matrimony, Uncle – you will be among the first to know. And now, if you please, may we return to your debts?"

"Fiend take it, I haven't come to pick your pockets, lad! I just thought it prudent to leave Town for a while."

"Bad as that, was it?"

"The duns at my door," confessed Sir Peregrine with a wry smile. "Beats me how they get wind. A fine thing it would be an' I started pandering to their paltry demands! You won't believe this, dear boy – I tried this new-fangled tailor . . . Ormskirk reckoned he was all the crack, so I let him make me a coat or two . . . fellow had the impudence to send in his bill! Coats weren't at all the thing either! Couldn't show my face at Boodle's in one of 'em! It's Weston for me from now on."

The Earl heard him out in patience, then repeated inexorably, "How much all told, Uncle?"

Sir Peregrine quoted a sum which his nephew accepted without blenching. "You had best furnish my secretary with a list of the whole," he said briefly.

"Oh, come now, Max! That's taking generosity too far! No objection to your settling my gaming debts – cursed embarrassing owing friends . . ."

"Quite so."

" . . . but you don't want to be troubling your head over the rest! I don't, I assure you."

The Earl pushed back his chair and stood up. "I pay all – or none, Uncle. The choice is yours. Now, shall we join the ladies?"

"As you will, dear boy," said his uncle philosophically. "And what will you do about this Hardman business?"

"For the moment," said the Earl, "nothing."

Chapter Seven

In spite of the setback, Felicity was determined that the children should not be denied their Christmas concert. An appeal to Mr. Becket brought a hasty coat of paint to the walls and temporary seating.

The concert was a triumph. Lord Stayne put in a last-minute appearance, also Sir Peregrine, Amaryllis, and Jamie. Their presence put everyone on their mettle and the children behaved beautifully. She was proud of them and though she kept a wary eye on Jamie and Lanny Price, they both seemed over-awed by the occasion.

Between Felicity and Ester, however, there was a distinct coolness. Ester had taken strong exception to having her affairs divulged to the Earl without her permission and no amount of persuasion would move her to seek his help.

Sir Peregrine stayed on for Christmas. There was quite a large house party, and with the prospect of some good shooting and congenial company, he was not hard to persuade. When the guests departed, he still showed little inclination to return to Town.

He liked to drive with Felicity in the gig. It was on one of these outings that they heard raised voices and came upon a knot of people milling around the boundary wall of Manor Court. The gate, with its grim warnings to trespassers, swung open. One or two women, hearing the gig, turned.

" 'Tis Miss Vale!"

"Oh, miss – it don't seem right! The lad don't know no better nor to do as 'e should . . ."

Felicity said sharply, "What lad?" She thought at once of Lanny. "Who is it?" she urged. "Who are you talking about?"

The woman who answered was big-eyed with her news. "It's young Willie Graham! The Captain has 'im fast in

158

there . . . stealin' he says."

Thrusting the reins into Uncle Perry's hands, Felicity sprang down and ran toward the gate, pushing her way through the onlookers.

Beyond the gate she stopped. There had been a light fall of snow, enough to cover the ground and powder the trees; it made an incongruously beautiful backdrop for a tableau assembled with the theatrical precision of high drama.

Captain Hardman, on his brute of a stallion, loomed above two small boys – Willie, passive and incurious under the hands of the head keeper, clutching to his chest a shining red ball; and, nearby, Geoffrey Hardman, stiff with outrage, yet with a suppressed air of gloating. Near the gate Ester was being restrained by a massive Negro and two other men watched the crowd for trouble.

Captain Hardman was addressing Ester in that light, expressionless voice and Felicity could tell that he was enjoying every minute.

" . . . you cannot deny the evidence of

your own eyes, madam. The ball belongs to my son – your boy has it in his possession – indeed he is loath to surrender it."

Felicity's heart sank. She saw at once what must have happened. She had been working very hard with Willie for the past few weeks, endeavoring to find some way through that wall of silent apathy; she sensed that he had taken to her and had used that faint thread of interest, painstakingly going over and over one simple theme – circles – all kinds of circles, including a red ball! Until this moment she was unsure whether she had made any progress, yet here surely was the proof; even in the midst of her dismay she could not restrain a thrill of elation.

She pressed forward until her way was barred.

"Let that child go this instant, Captain Hardman!"

He turned hard, pitiless eyes on her. "Ah, the schoolmarm! A propitious arrival. You are in time to witness the

160

punishment of one of your charges. You should govern them better, ma'am!"

"How can you talk of punishment? You know this child is not responsible for his actions."

"Then he must be made to learn that responsibility the hard way, idiot or no," he sneered.

"If that is how you feel," Felicity insisted desperately, "then take him before a magistrate."

The thin mouth twisted. "Before Stayne? What kind of justice would that produce, I wonder? No, Miss Vale – this is an affair between children; I have a fancy to keep it that way."

"The idiot stole my ball," smirked Geoffrey. "My father is going to let me beat him!"

Felicity stared at Hardman in disbelief. "But that is obscene! Surely even you would not encourage such sadistic brutality in your own son?"

One glance assured her that he would. His contempt flayed her like a lash. "Have a care, schoolmarm! You are trespassing on my land for the second time. I might yet be tempted to treat you in similar fashion!"

She flushed scarlet. Her eyes found Ester; anger mingled with terror in her face. Her own anger mounting, Felicity swung around on the crowd.

"Are you going to stand there and let this happen?"

Without waiting for answer she delivered a well-aimed elbow to her captor's midriff. Caught unawares, he doubled up in pain; she pushed him aside and ran to scoop Willie from the grasp of the momentarily disconcerted keeper.

Willie regarded her solemnly and slowly held out his hands. "Ball," he said quite distinctly.

For a moment everything stood still except her heart, which leapt with pride. She hugged him.

"Yes, dear, ball," she said. "But let us put it down now."

She took it from his unresisting fingers and let it drop to the ground.

"Fools! Dolts!" Captain Hardman

was nearly speechless with rage. "Seize her! Seize them both! Must I do everything myself?"

It was the first time Felicity had seen him off his horse – a vain strutting little man – but dangerous. She held the boy tighter as he advanced and from the corner of her eye saw the man she had winded and the keeper moving in from the other side.

There was an angry murmuring among the crowd. Above it came Sir Peregrine's voice, devoid of its customary geniality.

"Hold where you are, sirrah! Call off your bruisers if you value your miserable hide."

Felicity had completely forgotten him. She was never so glad to see anyone; her knees grew treacherously weak as he ranged himself alongside her, an elegant silver-mounted pistol held in a rock-steady hand.

Captain Hardman looked down its barrel – and up into Sir Peregrine's coldly cherubic face. He signaled his men to stand back.

"Who the devil are you?" His voice grated.

Sir Peregrine looked him over with an hauteur his nephew could not have bettered.

"I have not the least desire to converse with you, my man. Release these good people, and go about your business." With superb nonchalance he addressed Felicity. "Will you come, my dear . . . is this the young lad's mother? Come, ma'am."

The Negro released Ester. Behind them the Captain relieved his feelings by cuffing his son, who was shrieking with hysterical disappointment.

Coming upon Captain Hardman three days later in Stapleforth's Market Square, Lord Stayne dashed any hopes he might have entertained regarding the Graham cottage.

"There is a written agreement between Mrs. Graham and myself. In the event of her wishing to sell Ivy Cottage, I

164

have first refusal."

There was a petulance about the Captain's wrath. "Very clever, my lord. But I am not deceived. I perceive only too clearly whose hand is behind this turn of events. That Vale woman will regret the day she crossed my path with her radical arrogance and mischief-making! I don't tolerate it in my foundries – I certainly won't tolerate it on my doorstep from a soldier's upstart brat!"

"That will do, Captain!" The Earl's voice held the steely ring of authority. "The agreement is between Mrs. Graham and myself and no one else. Is that clear? Furthermore, I expect all pressures to cease forthwith!"

He saw the angry color creep up under the other man's skin and added meaningfully, "I am sure we understand one another."

When Felicity was summoned to the library she was uncertain what to expect. Lord Stayne had already expressed himself forcibly on the subject of the incident in Manor Court wood; she had only been prevented from taking issue with him by the intervention of Sir Peregrine.

"Let be, m'dear," he had counseled, drawing her away. "No sense brangling with Max when he's in a miff. Cuts up pretty nasty, I can tell you!"

She could divine little now from the Earl's expression. He frequently looked down his nose in that beetlebrowed fashion.

When he had allowed her ample time to grow uneasy, he observed with cutting sarcasm, "Strange. You do not have the look of a young woman bent upon self-destruction."

She stirred, frowning. "My lord?"

"I have warned you on more than one occasion, have I not, to refrain from antagonizing Captain Hardman?"

"Yes, but . . ."

"Permit me to finish, Miss Vale. Perhaps I have been at fault in allowing you free rein. It amused me to indulge you, and in many ways the experiment has proved beneficial. But you are too impetuous by far, ma'am. Your dealings with Hardman appear to border on the suicidal!"

"That is unfair! At no time have I set out to antagonize Captain Hardman!"

"Then it will astonish you to learn that he lays blame squarely at your door."

"And you?"

The Earl appeared to weigh his words. "I think you have been unwise."

"Because I interfered the other day . . ."

"I have already spoken my mind on that head!"

"Ah yes! It was none of my business . . . I should have passed by!" Felicity sprang to her feet and paced about the room. "Is that what you would have done, my lord?" When he didn't answer, she finished bitterly, "Well, I thank God your uncle thought differently!"

The candlelight threw up shadows and brought the scar on Stayne's cheekbone into sharp relief.

"Don't attempt to turn the argument,

Miss Vale. By interfering in a purely domestic dispute – a squabble between children upon private land – you placed yourself unquestionably in the wrong. Had Sir Peregrine not been on hand to intervene, you might have found yourself facing a very ugly situation."

Felicity swung around to face him, grasping the back of a chair.

"Domestic dispute?" she cried, ignoring his censure. "Is that how you see the obscenity of setting one boy on to beat another?"

"Oh, come now! You are over-dramatizing the whole thing. I doubt any lasting harm would have resulted."

Felicity met his eyes steadily. "If that is what you truly believe, my lord, then I am sorry for you."

The reproach disconcerted him. He said abruptly, "Sit down, Miss Vale."

"I thank you, sir, but, with your permission, I had far rather leave."

Exasperation flared anew. "Oh, for God's sake, girl – come down off your high ropes! Sit down. I have not done with you."

Felicity glared – and sat. The Earl watched her with a curious expression.

"Why do I bear with you, I wonder?" he murmured at last.

She supposed the question to be purely rhetorical, yet a sudden quirk moved her to remark, "I understood that you saw my refusal to be cowed as a challenge, my lord?"

"Did I say that? I must have been in my cups!" His look grew brooding. "If it is so, then I have served you a backhanded turn, I think – and must take some measure of responsibility for your subsequent handling of Captain Hardman."

"No, sir," she said firmly. "With respect, I cannot agree. I'll not hide behind you or anyone else. I shall always oppose people like Captain Hardman who assume that they have a God-given right to make their own rules and trample all resistance underfoot!"

The Earl sighed. "I see that I am wasting my breath. You are clearly destined to meet an untimely end."

Felicity smiled, uncertain of his mood.

"At least give me your word that you will stay out of Hardman's path. I did not exaggerate when I said that he blames you for his misfortunes. I have warned him off, but it is by no means certain that he will comply. He is not, as you will have realized, a rational man."

"No, indeed," she agreed readily. "I will certainly engage not to provoke him. But neither will I be silent if I see a need to speak."

Stayne grunted. "I suppose I must be satisfied with that."

She stood up. "May I go now, my lord?"

"Yes, Miss Vale – you may go," he said with a strong touch of irony. He moved to open the door for her. As she passed him, he restrained her for a moment more.

"Pray, do have a care," he urged in an

odd sort of voice. "If anything were to happen to you, I have a curious notion that we should all be the worse for it."

Chapter Eight

Sir Peregrine's going seemed to entail an even greater upheaval than his arrival.

His genial, good-natured presence was sorely missed. Amaryllis soon fell into a fit of the blue megrims; she sighed a lot and complained incessantly of the inclement weather and of the drafts. In this, at least, she was justified, for in spite of numerous fires kept halfway up the chimneys, the drafts whistled persistently through the vaulted hall and up the grand staircase; they wheezed through the window cracks and under bedchamber doors to flirt with the hangings.

Her complaints embraced Stapleforth's lack of amenities – no assembly rooms, no theater, not so much as a lending library. Her headaches became more frequent, and when the Earl finally lost patience and spoke sharply to her one evening, she burst into tears and fled the table.

Behind her, an uncomfortable silence reigned. Felicity, uncertain whether to follow her cousin or stay, was impatient with both parties; with Amaryllis for carrying on in a manner calculated to irritate her brother-in-law, and with the Earl for his easily provoked intolerance.

He said austerely, "I apologize for precipitating one of my sister-in-law's tantrums, Miss Vale. It was clumsy of me, when I am well aware what must be the object of these frequent displays of histrionics."

"Do they have an object, my lord?" Felicity feigned innocence and received a hard stare for her pains.

"I am fully aware that before my uncle departed he fostered certain aspirations within Amaryllis . . . that she might, in fact, go to London for the season. Since I hold the purse strings, I imagine she is hoping to convince me that she is in sore need of a change."

"Then put her out of her misery, my lord, and tell her she may go."

Stayne raised a haughty eyebrow. "I beg your pardon?"

"Oh, forgive me. Of course, it is not for me to presume to offer an opinion."

"I don't recall you have ever let that stop you!" he said dryly.

"Well, you obviously mean to let Amaryllis go to London . . ."

"Do I? Why should I?"

"Because she is a fish out of water down here in the country. And because it will make her very happy," she finished simply.

The Earl paused, his glass halfway to his lips, and surveyed her over the rim. "And that seems to you sufficient reason?"

"I cannot think of a better one, sir. Can you?"

He raised the glass to her with the ghost of a smile. "No, Miss Vale. Offhand, I cannot."

And so, before the Earl set out for Ascot two days later, he informed

Amaryllis that she might go to London in the spring and that she might charge all expenses to him.

Amaryllis, overcome by his sudden generosity and mildness of manner, began to stammer incoherent thanks, but was cut short with the recommendation that she direct any thanks toward her cousin.

Headaches forgotten, she rushed up to Felicity's room where she grabbed her startled cousin by the waist and waltzed her recklessly around until, in the confined space, they collapsed in a heap on the bed. Amaryllis disentangled herself first and sat up.

"Only think of it, Fliss! London! For the whole season! Oh, I cannot believe it!" She fell at once to planning her wardrobe. "I shall need new dresses . . . I declare, I haven't a stitch to wear! What a happy coincidence that I had those new French journals from Lucinda . . . they have the very latest fashions!"

Felicity, still catching her breath, protested that she had whole cupboards full of beautiful clothes, an observation which drew a charming moue.

"Oh, but they are all quite old! A fine thing it would be an I appeared as a frump!"

Felicity gurgled with laughter. "A physical impossibility, my dear. You could never look other than wholly ravishing!"

Amaryllis accepted the compliment without demur. "Well, I am determined to be of the first stare. Max has been quite astonishingly generous! What did he mean about directing my thanks to you?"

"Did he say that? What an extraordinary man he is! I simply suggested that it would be a good idea for you to go to London, with little hope that he would take note."

"Well, he has – and I do thank you, dear Fliss. Will Ester help with the sewing, do you think? She is so much busier these days."

"I'm sure she will. I'll help, too."

"You are much too good to me," said

Amaryllis, with unusual perception. "I daresay you are quite as much in need of a change as I." Her eyes brightened. "Come to London with me. You spend far too much time slaving over those wretched children – it really isn't necessary, you know. I'm sure Ester could run the school... and you've made your point with Stayne – he has long since ceased to think of you as hanging out for favors."

Felicity winced at the unfortunate choice of words.

"Thank you, but I would rather not trade on his lordship's good nature. Besides, I enjoy my school – and now that Ester is become so adept, I am able to devote more of my time to the backward children."

"Oh well, as you please." Amaryllis gave an impatient shrug, unable and unwilling to understand such odd compulsions. The boy of Ester's, for instance. The child was repulsive! How could Felicity bear to have him follow her around with his peculiarly vacant stare! She shuddered.

While Lord Stayne was away, Jamie's tutor arrived to take up his position. The Reverend Aloysius Burnett was a shy, angular young man whose boney nose and finger ends seemed to be forever pinched bright pink by the cold. He came with the highest references and settled into the household with such gentle unobtrusiveness that Felicity at first doubted his ability to handle a boy as high-spirited as Jamie. However, it quickly became apparent that his gentleness cloaked a firmness of purpose allied to a keen intellect, which soon proved more than a match for the most determined small boy.

It was unfortunate that almost within days of his arrival Jamie went down with the measles. The disease started in the school and spread rapidly. When Lanny Price succumbed, Felicity knew it must only be a matter of time before Jamie followed suit.

Dr. Belvedere insisted that the school be closed and Felicity wasn't sorry, for

Jamie as a patient proved to be a full-time job – and one that devolved almost entirely upon her, with Rose Hibberd's help.

To give Amaryllis her due, she did try, but her nerves did not stand up well to the rigors of the sickroom; her tearful ministrations had an unfortunate effect upon the invalid, and more often than not culminated in the onset of a migraine, when only one of Felicity's tisane's would bring comfort.

Most afternoons Felicity did manage to get a little fresh air. She usually rode into the village with a few delicacies begged from Mrs. Hudson for the worst-hit families.

After one such visit Felicity encountered the Lipscombe carriage coming away from Cheynings. Her heart sank as Mrs. Lipscombe, muffled to the eyebrows in sable, let down the window and beckoned.

"Miss Vale! We have left cards."

Felicity reined Starlight in alongside the carriage. The young horse, with the fidgets scarcely shaken out of her legs, shied nervously at the high, querulous voice. Felicity ran a soothing hand along her neck and mustered a smile.

"Mrs. Lipscombe. I am sorry to have been out. Cavanah will have told you of our troubles, I daresay. Will you not come back with me now? You will find Amaryllis a trifle indisposed, but I am sure she would be much cheered by a visit from Miss Lipscombe."

The atmosphere cooled. Mrs. Lipscombe was not pleased to find this upstart girl so much in charge; even Cavanah, it would seem, took his tone from her.

"I cannot permit it, Miss Vale. Indeed, I am astonished to hear you suggest such a visit."

There was amusement in Felicity's voice. "It is only the measles, ma'am – a simple childish ailment, nothing more."

Lucinda leaned forward, clutching her reticule. "I have not had the measles, Miss Vale."

Felicity examined the empty, flawless

features framed exquisitively in ruby velvet, and felt a momentary pang of sympathy.

"My dear Lucinda has a most delicate constitution," her mother was saying in quelling tones. "I could not think of exposing her to the risk. Were Lord Stayne here," she added meaningfully, "I feel sure he would endorse my decision!"

Felicity almost snorted aloud. If Stayne were home, the old dragon would be pushing her daughter in at the door! She swallowed these unladylike sentiments and said mildly: "I hardly think a few words with Amaryllis likely to endanger Miss Lipscombe's health, ma'am, but of course you must do as you think fit."

She made light of it to Amaryllis.

"Well, I'm sure I don't care!" Amaryllis said crossly. "I don't think I could have listened to Lucinda boring on forever about her latest stay in Norfolk and all the balls she will have attended! That sort of thing is very well if one has no

181

responsibilities!"

These observations were so totally out of character that Felicity was hard put to it not to laugh. But there were dark circles under the gentian blue eyes. "I daresay you will think that a very strange remark for me to be making?"

"I think nothing of the kind," said Felicity gently. "Your sentiments are everything I would expect in you. Jamie must naturally come first in your thoughts, but a little relaxation – a little taking out of yourself, would perhaps be beneficial."

"No, no! I can think of nothing else . . . why, he hardly knew me just now . . . when I remember how I used to complain of his constant chatter! If only he will get well. . . . Oh, why is Dr. Belvedere not here?"

Her words were punctuated by sobs and Felicity's heart ached for her.

"You must not worry so. The doctor will come, but he is very busy at present and there is little more he can do. The fever must run its course."

But the fever continued to mount and with it his mother's panic.

"I'm so afraid," she sobbed. "I know you all wish to spare my feelings, but I feel sure he is going to . . ." she pressed a hand convulsively to her mouth.

"Oh, good gracious! Nothing of the kind!" cried Felicity. "By tomorrow or the next day you will be laughing at your fears!"

She did not add that Mary Perkins down in the village had died that very morning – and she hoped that no one would be so thoughtless as to mention the tragedy in her cousin's hearing. The Perkinses were a sickly family, after all, particularly little Mary, who at eight had been under-sized and dogged by a persistent racking cough. If this had not taken her, doubtless something else would have.

Felicity persuaded Amaryllis to go and rest, " . . . you look quite worn out. And Jamie will need you fresh and cheerful when he is over this little setback."

Amaryllis went, with a backward glance into the darkened room where her son turned his head restlessly away from Rose Hibberd's cooling sponge. The curtains were drawn against the light, which hurt his eyes.

"You will let me know if . . . Oh, Felicity, why does Max not come? It is two days since I sent word!"

Her original insistence on sending for Lord Stayne had surprised Felicity, but this heartfelt cry now found an echo in her own thoughts, for somehow the Earl's very air of omniscience was guaranteed to exercise a calming influence.

It was well past midnight when he did come. The first she knew was when he stood in the doorway, his body tense, his face in shadow. A screen shielded the bed from the single lamp where Felicity sat mending one of Jamie's shirts.

She put it down and came softly across the room.

"Miss Vale." His voice lacked its usual incisiveness. "May I come in?"

She stood aside to let him pass. He stood, frowning at her as though he hardly recognized her in the simple cream wrapper, with her hair brushed free. She met his look and found her heart beating a little faster.

"Why are you here?" he asked. "Is there not a hired nurse?"

"No, sir. We are managing very well without. But I am glad you are come."

"My sister-in-law's note was somewhat incoherent?" His eyes lifted to the screened bed. "Jamie . . .?"

Felicity's matter-of-fact voice was reassuring. "He has been quite ill, but he has come through the crisis splendidly. Dr. Belvedere says he will soon be feeling more the thing."

They crossed together to the bed where the small boy lay fast asleep.

"He looks . . . thinner," said his uncle abruptly.

"Perhaps . . . a little, but that is soon put right." They moved softly away again into the pool of lamplight. "It is Amaryllis who needs you."

The Earl looked skeptical. "You need not tell me. My sister-in-law has spent most of her time prostrate with the vapors!"

Felicity shook her head. "This time you wrong her, my lord. Oh, I'm not saying she has been much use in the sickroom; her nerves, as you know, are not of the strongest."

Stayne snorted.

"But she has tried! You would be astonished, I think, to know how much she has tried!"

"I am delighted to hear it," said the Earl. "But I know to whom we owe our gratitude for Jamie's safe deliverance – and much else besides – these days past. Your resourcefulness has made a great impression upon Cavanah – a veritable tower of strength were, I believe, the words he used!"

Tiredness made Felicity oversensitive to the ever-present sarcasm. "I am sorry if you think I have exceeded my position . . ."

"Good God!" Stayne grasped her arm

and swung her around. "Miss Vale – in my somewhat clumsy fashion I am trying to thank you!"

"Oh!" She blinked up at him. There were tears glinting on her lashes, as there had been on the first day they had met, and the soft lamplight was making a nimbus of her hair. He found himself wanting very much to touch it.

Felicity wondered why he did not let her go. He was looking at her so strangely that she caught her breath. How long they stood – or what might have been the outcome – she was never to know; there was a sound from the doorway and they turned to find Amaryllis, in a trailing peignoir, clutching at the post.

"Max!"

He moved and caught her as she fell against him. Only when she had been fully reassured and had seen for herself that Jamie was sleeping, would she allow herself to be led back to her own room. The Earl's gentleness and patience were so at odds with his customary brusqueness that Felicity, tired as she was, found all her preconceived notions in a turmoil.

"I am taking Amaryllis to her bed now, Miss Vale," he said. "And then I intend to find someone to sit with Jamie for the remainder of the night so that you, too, may take a much-needed rest."

"There is no need . . ."

"I disagree, my dear young lady. There is every need. You are quite clearly worn out."

"I am nothing of the kind! I beg you will leave matters alone, my lord. All has been most carefully arranged so that we each take our turn. Besides, I would prefer to be here if Jamie should wake."

"Miss Vale," returned the Earl with equal determination, "you have had things very much your own way these days past, but I am here now and I believe I am still master in my own house!"

Amaryllis looked from one to the other, tearful and bewildered.

"Oh, but Max . . . you cannot know . . . Felicity has been so good . . . so truly good! You can have no idea . . .

I do not know how I should have gone on without her."

"On the contrary, I trust Miss Vale is in no doubt of my gratitude?"

Faced with so arbitrary an appeal, Felicity capitulated – and was rewarded by an unexpectedly warm smile.

"There – you see? There is no difficulty."

Within three days Jamie was displaying an unbelievable amount of energy and was being indulged by almost everyone until he stood in danger of being thoroughly spoiled. Even his uncle, who called him a noisome, pampered brat, gave the lie to his words by spending many a long hour at his bedside fashioning small boats out of paper.

It was the Earl who carried him down to the drawing room at last with the doctor's permission – and having performed his duty, showed little inclination to leave. When, an hour or so later, Mrs. and Miss Lipscombe were announced, they walked in upon a most affecting family scene.

Jamie and his mother, together with Felicity and Lord Stayne, were sitting on the floor before a blazing log fire arguing over a game of spillikins which seemed to involve a great deal of noise and general hilarity.

From the set of Mrs. Lipscombe's mouth, the scene afforded her little pleasure, but she mellowed slightly as the Earl came quickly to his feet. He greeted them with punctilious good manners, bade them to be seated, and suggested that Cavanah might bring a tea tray.

Amaryllis, flushed from the fire and not particularly pleased by the intrusion, stood up more slowly.

"I had not expected to see you, ma'am," she said with a touch of waspishness. "Or you, Lucinda. Especially you! Are you not afraid to be in the same room with my Jamie? He is not yet fully recovered, you know."

Lucinda flushed and watched with some trepidation as Jamie showed every sign of wishing to be intimate and had to be restrained by Felicity.

A flurry of hail splattered the windows, icily enhancing the look Mrs. Lipscombe directed at Felicity, for so obviously carrying tales to her cousin. She covered her daughter's discomfiture with a light laugh.

"My dear Amaryllis," she confided archly, "you must not blame Lucinda for being a dutiful daughter, it was I who held her back – impelled by a strong maternal urge to protect, which I am sure you must allow to be understandable? Do you not allow it to be so, Lord Stayne?"

"Oh, quite," said the Earl politely. "A very natural instinct, ma'am."

"Quite so. I knew you must understand. But Mr. Lipscombe is made of sterner stuff than I. He has a strong sense of duty. 'Only consider, madam,' he said to me, 'Only consider what a comfort your daughter's presence must afford Mrs. Delamere at this difficult time. Such charitable considerations must outweigh all risks!' And so I have suffered my scruples to be overset."

It was unfortunate that she chanced to glance at Felicity just as the latter was quite wickedly hazarding a guess as to when the news of Lord Stayne's return had reached the Lipscombe household. She could not accurately divine the girl's thoughts, but knew open insolence when she saw it. Her nostrils flared, making her resemblance to a horse more marked.

"I understand the disease emanated from your school, Miss Vale."

Before Felicity could take issue, the Earl interposed smoothly: "Who can tell where such epidemics have their origins, ma'am. They are common enough in all conscience. My brother and I seldom mixed with other children, yet I remember we took every childish ailment without exception."

Jamie listened with absorbed interest, and not wishing to be excluded from a topic upon which he was so obviously an expert, now entered the conversation with enthusiasm.

"I had the measles much worse than my friend, Lanny Price, Cousin F'licity said so! I had a rash all over, but it has quite gone now. Would you like to see?"

He advanced in the friendliest way upon the visitors, already tugging at the neck of his nightgown beneath the bright red dressing gown.

Mrs. Lipscombe uttered a little shriek and Lucinda turned pale. Felicity swooped on the miscreant and lifted him off his feet.

"Thank you, Jamie – but no. I think you have been downstairs quite long enough for your first day. Say good afternoon now and we will go."

"But I'm not in the least bit tired, Cousin F'licity, truly! I thought we were to play another game."

Lord Stayne took Jamie from Felicity's arms and strode swiftly to the door.

"Tomorrow," he said firmly.

Outside, his eyes met Felicity's. He swung the boy high onto his shoulder.

"Abominable wretch! Putting us all to the blush in that way."

"I didn't do anything!" Jamie objected. "I don't want to go back to bed."

"You'll do as you're told, young man," ordered his uncle, setting him down in the nursery doorway. "Be good for Miss Vale and perhaps I will come up later and teach you to play chess."

"Will you?" Jamie demanded eagerly. "Promise?"

"We shall see."

The small boy eyed them both consideringly. "Uncle Max – why do you call cousin F'licity 'Miss Vale' all the time? Don't you like her?"

The Earl's brows came together and Felicity felt ready to sink.

"Jamie!"

"Well – Mamma calls you F'licity, and so does Uncle Perry."

"That is quite different," she argued, wishing desperately that Jamie might suddenly be struck dumb.

"I don't see why!" the small voice continued with unwavering tenacity. "Uncle Max has known you much longer than Uncle Perry, and besides..."

194

"Jamie – that will do!" Her face now scarlet, Felicity grasped his shoulders and propeled him into his room without further ado.

To her dismay, the Earl followed; catching his eye she was thrown into further confusion by the derisive enjoyment lurking therein.

"What Miss Vale is no doubt shy of pointing out, my revolting nephew," he said smoothly, "is that the nature of our . . . er, relationship, being more professional than social, precludes any such intimacy – indeed, it would sit ill with the local schoolmistress to be thus familiarly addressed by her employer and patron. There," he turned to Felicity, "have I explained the matter to your satisfaction, ma'am?"

"No, you have not, my lord!" she cried, torn between laughter and outrage. "What a nonsense! As though I would ever entertain such pretentious and . . . idiotish notions!" He was so obviously gratified by her reaction that she was moved to add loftily, "I am sure your lordship is quite at liberty to address me howsoever you choose!"

The Earl, seeing Jamie's air of puzzlement, put out a hand to ruffle the dark curls.

"There's a handsome offer, my lad," he said with a grin. Turning to Felicity his manner became gently mocking. "Thank you, Miss Vale – I may just take you up on it sometime!"

Chapter Nine

March seemed bent on proving itself both turbulent and destructive. As the gales gathered momentum, Felicity was not sorry that the school was closed, though she expected the doctor's permission to reopen any day. Most of the children were fully recovered and there had been no new cases for two weeks.

She found herself owning to a twinge of guilt that she had so much enjoyed her time at home – for she now thought of Cheynings as home. The weather had kept everyone in a great deal more than usual and had served to draw them all closer together as a family. Even Lord Stayne had maintained an unusually sanguine disposition, prompting Amaryllis to remark that she could not remember his ever being so consistently good-humored for so long. Jamie was once more fighting fit and consigned to the care of his tutor.

With so much time at their disposal, the sewing had gone forward steadily. Amaryllis sat up in bed one morning, drinking chocolate and admiring the colorful and diaphanous accumulation of finery. The door opened to admit Felicity, dressed for riding.

"Goodness! You are never going out?"

Felicity grinned. "Oh pooh! It would take more than a bit of wind to frighten me off . . . and the worst does seem to be over. I don't believe I've ever been so long confined indoors in my life! I cannot bear it a moment longer!"

"Yes, but only consider the blessings of such weather. The Lipscombes have not called for two whole weeks!"

Felicity laid her riding hat and whip on the end of the bed and perched beside them, glancing curiously at her cousin.

"You really don't mind, do you? I thought you and Lucinda such good friends?"

"And now you think me very fickle." Amaryllis pouted. "Well, I am fickle, dear Fliss. I daresay you would like to think I have changed, but I haven't. I never liked Lucinda that much, only there was very little choice of company when I first came here, and we were thrown together by cause of Mrs. Lipscombe's determination that Lucinda should marry Maxim."

Felicity knew a curious pang. "And will she, do you suppose?"

"Oh yes, I should think so," was the careless reply. "Max doesn't really care for women, you know, so Lucinda will do as well as the next; she looks well enough and is very biddable when it suits her. She will make Max an adequate wife."

Amaryllis smiled a little maliciously. "Only Mamma is having more trouble than she imagined bringing him up to scratch! She expected her connection with the Wellesleys would weigh with him more than it has."

Felicity longed to protest that Lucinda would bore Stayne silly within a month, but the words choked her. Instead she jumped up, set her hat very firmly on her head, snatched up her whip, and almost ran from the room, leaving Amaryllis to wonder what had brought the snapping lights into her cousin's eyes.

Outside, the worst of the wind had indeed died down, but the trees and bushes were still alive with it and the devastated gardens bore witness to its passing. Several gardeners were hard at work clearing up.

In the stable yard there was an atmosphere. The Earl's curricle stood waiting; the famous grays, perhaps affected by the wildness in the air, rolled their eyes and strained restively against the combined attentions of two grooms.

Benson was almost absent-minded in his greeting, and young Percy, resplendent in his blue and gold livery, sidled constantly to the archway to stare up the drive – and hardly heard when Felicity spoke.

"Is something wrong, Benson?"

He jumped. "Oh, Miss Vale – 'tis you!" He blew his nose noisily. "I don't rightly know, miss. It's his lordship – rode out over an hour ago, he did – down to Long Meadow to inspect one of them old elm trees Mr. Becket reckoned ought to come down. He said he'd be back within the hour, and I was to 'ave the horses put to." He buttoned and unbuttoned his coat nervously. "Well, you'll allow it ain't like his lordship to keep such prime goers a-standing?"

"No . . .o," conceded Felicity, "but any number of things might have detained him, you know. Perhaps you should . . . no, wait a minute . . . I believe this is him now."

She had hardly finished speaking when the Earl's stallion came thundering under the arch, riderless and trailing his rein.

Percy, his eyes ablaze, his nose red with cold, charged after him.

"What did I tell you, Benson? Trouble! I could smell it! We got to get

201

out there right away!"

Felicity's heart gave a lurch, but she said calmly enough, "Lord Stayne won't thank you for being overhasty, you know. Vulcan might have panicked."

Percy threw her a pitying look. "That's gammon, miss – and you know it, beggin' your pardon. That horse wouldn't never run out on the guv'nor, no matter what . . . leastways, not without cause."

"The lad's right, miss," said Benson heavily. "Something must have happened . . . there's blood here on Vulcan's ear. Saddle me a horse, Dan – on the double, lad, and we'd best have a wagon along, too – just in case!"

Against her will, Felicity found their fear contagious. "Surely, if you consider the matter urgent, you have a much faster vehicle here, ready and waiting?"

There was a shocked silence throughout the yard.

Percy's mouth dropped open. "Miss! You ain't never suggestin' . . .?"

Felicity gestured impatiently toward

202

the curricle, where the grays were now stamping and showing the whites of their eyes.

"Well, isn't it obvious? Benson – you must be quite well able to manage them?"

"Drive his lordship's cattle, miss?" Benson's voice was a croak. "You're never serious, Miss Vale?"

"Of course I'm serious. This is no time for levity."

"Then I'm sorry, miss," he said bluntly. "I ain't precisely squeamish, you understand – but then I ain't hellbent on committing suicide, neither – and suicide, near as dammit, is what it 'ud amount to if I was to do as you suggest. You wouldn't know, miss," he explained kindly, "never having been on the wrong end of his lordship's tongue, so to speak. Meself – I'd as soon face a line of fire, any day!" A slight shudder shook the sturdy frame.

Felicity found such timidity vaguely irritating. "Oh really! How can you be thinking of yourself when Lord Stayne

might at this very moment be lying un-
conscious?"

"That's as may be, Miss Vale, but, if
it's all the same to you, I'll harness the
wagon, for less'n he's dead, which God
forbid, I ain't chancin' it! Very perticler,
is his lordship! If I was to tool that little
lot without his permission – and them
fresh as they are – I'd be out of a job
quicker'n you could spit, savin' your
presence, miss!"

She was obliged to admit that Benson
could not be expected to put his job at
risk. If there were only someone else . . .

Her glance strayed speculatively toward the waiting curricle and she
experienced the sudden thrill of anticipation tinged with fear which always
came to her in the face of a challenge . . .
Dare she? Oh, but she would dearly love
to try! Even as the idea crystalized, she
knew she would do it – and the decision
was not solely governed by concern for
Stayne.

A clamor of protest followed her as
she climbed purposefully into the pre-

carious driving seat and gathered up the reins.

"You must all do as you please," she declared, looking down on a semicircle of distraught faces. "To my mind, this is no time to turn chicken-hearted! Are you coming, Percy?"

"Oh Gawd, miss! Don't do it!" The young tiger's face was screwed up in an agony of indecision. "I ... c-can't ... don't ... ask me! I ain't never been driven by a female afore!" The cry seemed wrung from him.

"Please yourself," snapped Felicity, stifling her own growing qualms. Somehow, sitting all alone, the ground appeared much farther away. She took a firm grip on the reins and on her fast-evaporating courage. "Right, my lads," she ordered in business-like fashion. "You may let the horses go."

The stable boys threw a last frightened glance at Benson, but he was busy bellowing for his own horse and merely shrugged, knowing himself beaten, so they let go – and with the sweet smell of freedom in their nostrils, the leaders sprang forward.

In the last split second Percy leaped for his perch, where he hung on, petrified, alternately shouting advice and wailing that they would be hurled into the first ditch and "killed sure!"

Felicity scarcely heard him. She suddenly found herself facing several very pressing hazards all at the same time – not the least of which was the unpleasant prospect of having her arms wrenched from their sockets as she struggled to contain the grays' headlong progress, while resisting the very natural temptation to drag back so hard on the rein as to damage their delicate mouths.

Even her worry about Stayne paled before the enormity of what she was doing, yet a tiny corner of her brain was responding to the memory of skills painstakingly learned on the dusty streets of Lisbon years back; instinct sent the thong of the whip whistling forward to flick the leaders and instinct prompted her to exert just the correct amount of pressure to execute the sharp right-hand turn which would take them down toward Long Meadow.

But for the most part, reality had ceased to have any meaning; these rhythmic, straining bodies compounded of muscle and sinew, beautiful and exhilarating though they were to behold, were not horses at all; they were flying emissaries – self-willed, misbegotten winged messengers of Satan bent upon destruction. And if they didn't annihilate her, then at the end of it the Earl most certainly would!

As though endorsing these gloomy presentiments, Percy's voice quavered behind her. "He'll massacre us, for sure! A female driving the Guvnor's grays ... and me a party to it! Oh, oh ... I'll never hold me head up again!"

"For heaven's sake, hold your tongue, boy!" snapped Felicity.

Bare branches clawed, hedgerow and thicket flashed by, and Percy's voice rose again.

"There he is, miss! Oh, and mercy on us, isn't he on his own two feet? Not even half killed! Nothing can save us now!" With which fateful pronouncement he subsided into petrified silence.

Felicity, mastering an overwhelming attack of nerves on seeing that ominously still, upright figure awaiting them, brought the team to a commendable halt. Percy scrambled down without a word and ran to the horses' heads.

The ensuing silence stretched to deafening proportions. Felicity sat, her hands gripped in her lap; now that the excitement was over, she couldn't stop them shaking. The realization that the Earl was not after all prostrate afforded her little relief; quite illogically, she had almost rather they had found him mortally injured. At least, she thought resentfully, that would have provided some justification for her actions.

Unable to stave off the moment any longer, she raised her gaze from contemplation of her hands and encountered so blistering a shaft of fury from those

black eyes that she instinctively re-
coiled.

"What in thunder **do you suppose you
are about?**"

**Although he stood erect, she saw that
he supported himself against a tree. Behind him a rotten branch had been torn
violently from the massive trunk and
hung by a shred of bark, creaking
mournfully as the wind moved it.**

**Blood was oozing gently from a gash
on the Earl's temple and he was very
white about the mouth, but whether
from his injury or sheer temper Felicity
wasn't sure.**

**She was out of the curricle in an in-
stant and at his side.**

"Oh indeed, you are hurt!"

His arm stiffened under her clasp.

**"I – am – awaiting – your explan-
ation, madam." Each word seemed bit-
ten off. "You do have – an explan-
ation?"**

**"Yes, of course. Vulcan came back,
you see..." she began inadequately.
"I... that is, we thought you must**

have . . . had an accident."

The excuses rang lamely, even in her own ears. The sound of horses provided a momentary distraction. Benson came galloping into view, followed by one of the grooms driving a light wagonette. The Earl's frigid glance lifted to take in this latest contingent of the rescue party.

"I see. Your corporate concern is . . . touching!"

Again Felicity noticed the staccato speech. She looked at him closely. The scar on his cheek showed tight and puckered against his extreme pallor and his mouth was compressed in a thin line, but again, whether this was due to the gash on his head or anger, she couldn't tell. She noticed that he still held to the tree.

Benson dismounted and came across, exchanging a hurried but expressive glance with Felicity.

"My lord – are you all right?"

"No, Benson – I am not all right."

Benson looked closer. "Aye – well, that's a nasty looking cut and no mistake. We'd best get you home, m'lord, and one of my lads can go for Dr. Belvedere."

He looked unhappily from the curricle to the wagonette, seemingly at a loss. His lordship, however, was curtly decisive.

"Don't talk like a fool, man! I need no doctor – and I need no help. Take that... conveyance away. I shall have plenty to say to you later."

"You must not blame Benson for what has happened," said Felicity quickly. "He did try to dissuade me."

The Earl might not have heard. Master and servant looked steadily at one another, then Benson moved heavily back to his horse.

"Aye, well – you'll do as you please, I suppose," he mumbled.

"I will. And you may take Percy with you. He is at present skulking behind my grays."

Percy showed a red, aggrieved face. "Doin' me job, I am, Guv – looking after your bleedin' horses!"

211

"Thank you, Percy, but I believe we may dispense with your help." The Earl's tone was cuttingly sarcastic. "You have helped enough for one day! The grays will not bolt, I think."

The sorry cavalcade departed, leaving Felicity alone with Lord Stayne – he, thin-lipped and obviously exercising the tightest control – she, disheveled and flying bright flags of color in her cheeks.

Neither seemed willing to break the silence. In the end, nervousness made Felicity plunge flippantly: "I suppose you have sent them all away so that you may quarrel with me undisturbed!"

Even as the words tumbled out, she would have given anything to bite them back. Without quite meeting his eye, she rushed on, floundering in acute mortification: "I didn't mean ... that is, I'm truly ... sorry, my lord. My behavior must ... seem unpardonable ..."

"Unpardonable!" He gave the word a savage emphasis. "Yes, madam – I would certainly say unpardonable. I believe I shall be a long time forgiving you for this day's work!"

His total rejection of her clumsily worded apology rankled; her first instinct was to meet fire with fire, but a niggling awareness of the enormity of her crime obliged her to attempt conciliation.

"Oh come, my lord," she urged, "was it so very bad? No real harm has been done, after all."

"No harm, you say! No harm that a young woman employed by me in a position of some responsibility disports herself like a mindless hoyden before my servants!" His raking glance was contemptuous. "If you could but see yourself at this moment, madam, you might think otherwise."

Felicity was stung; for the first time she became aware that her hair had been torn from its pins by the wind and was spilling down her back in a most unruly fashion. With angry, resentful tears locking her throat, she gathered it with impatient fingers and crammed it under her hat in a gesture of defiance.

The Earl watched with an air of grim vindication. "However – deplorable though I consider your want of decorum – it is in the matter of my horses that I find you to be most glaringly at fault! To have commandeered my curricle as you did, against all advice, can only be termed a flagrant act of vandalism."

"Oh, but I . . ."

"Be silent, madam! I must be thankful, I suppose, that you have not succeeded in maiming my grays beyond recall. As it is, thanks to your desire to emulate Letty Lade, I shall be surprised if I do not find their mouths sawn to pieces!"

"How dare you!" This time Felicity was too angry to be silenced. "How dare you be so tyrannical and . . . pompous! Yes, pompous! Do you imagine for one moment that I would attempt to drive your wretched horses if I didn't think myself competent? You have not troubled to check their condition!" She was well launched into the attack now and past caring about the consequences.

"Take a good look at them, my lord. Do they seem badly winded – or in any way discomforted? Look well, and if you can find so much as a strained fetlock or a bruised mouth, then I will endure your strictures! Furthermore, even if you did, which you won't, it would not excuse your base ingratitude, which I find a poor recompense for what was a sincere, if impetuous, concern for your well-being!"

It was a long and, toward the end, somewhat involved speech. By the end she was so far convinced of the hopelessness of expecting or receiving any quarter that, for good measure, she added a final inflammatory thrust.

"And if you think so much of your precious grays, my lord, you ought not to keep them standing about in the cold when you might as easily rip up my character at home!"

She supposed that rage had finally deprived the Earl of speech until his hand slowly loosed its hold on the tree and he took a step forward, muttering thickly, "Yes, of course . . . you are right . . ."

And then, under her horrified gaze, he began to sway alarmingly, his face the color of parchment.

"Oh glory!" Felicity's anger evaporated instantly. She flew to his side and for the first time in her life thanked a merciful providence that had built her on such generous lines; she eased a strong young shoulder beneath his oxter and clasped his arm around her neck.

"There now, dear sir – hang on. For pity's sake, don't you dare swoon on me!"

A feeble laugh shook him. "No chance!" he muttered.

He was almost dead weight, but Felicity managed to struggle as far as the tree, where he leaned back with eyes closed.

She eyed him in growing alarm, wishing fervently that he had not been so precipitate in dispatching Benson.

"Brandy, my lord? Do you have brandy?"

He seemed to sigh. "Left ... hand pocket."

She found the flask and watched him drink. After a few moments he opened his eyes. "That's better ... I shall do, presently."

His color was indeed improving a little. She asked diffidently: "Do you feel strong enough to walk to your curricle, my lord? I think the sooner you are home, the better."

"Don't fuss, Miss Vale."

"No, sir."

A few more minutes passed; to Felicity it seemed an eternity until he said abruptly, "Give me your arm, now. We will go."

He climbed into the waiting curricle and sank back with a sigh. Felicity followed quickly, reaching for the reins.

Stayne gathered himself with an effort. "Thank you, Miss Vale. I will drive."

"Oh, my lord, be sensible!" she urged, worry making her less than tactful. It earned her a withering look. He held out his hand and without further argument she relinquished the ribbons.

For a while all went well; then he misjudged a turn badly and swore as he corrected his error. Felicity sat tense, gritting her teeth, vowing she would not interfere again.

A few yards more and without warning the Earl brought the grays to a halt. He slumped in his seat, his hands dropping between his knees, his breath coming in quick, shallow bursts.

"I fear . . . you are right, Miss Vale . . . any farther and I shall bring us to grief . . ."

Felicity had seen the symptoms many times. She conquered the shake in her voice, took the reins, and said matter-of-factly, "That would be a pity, sir. I daresay you have a little concussion, you know – from the blow you took."

"Quite possibly," he said, and shut his eyes.

When they reached the stable yard, Benson's surly apprehension turned to concern. Under Felicity's watchful eye he helped his lordship down and together they assisted him toward the house. Here, Cavanah, having been forewarned, waited with a strong, young footman. This was too much for the Earl. He straightened up and disposed of them all in a pithy, idiomatic sentence, before steering a lone, if somewhat erratic, course toward the library.

Felicity followed quickly on his heels, giving Cavanah a number of low-voiced instructions.

"You don't think perhaps the doctor, Miss Vale?"

She smiled reassuringly. "I think not – for the present, at least."

A footman came into the library, bearing a tray which he laid down silently on a table close to the Earl's chair. He inquired if there was anything further Miss Vale would be wanting?

Felicity glanced at the tray and shook her head. The footman withdrew and she began to wring out a cloth in the hot water.

"I am going to bathe your head, my

lord," she said with deliberate cheerfulness. "Cavanah will send your valet presently to assist you to your room. I expect you will feel much more the thing when you are rested."

"The devil I will!" he retorted. "You are too busy ma'am. I shall do very well if you will just go away and leave me be."

"Presently, sir, when I have finished."

She continued to dab at the congealed blood. He winced as she probed gently at the jagged gash, lest there be any hidden splinters.

"If you will just be still, sir . . ."

"Dammit, Miss Vale! I am not Jamie!"

"No, my lord." She smothered a smile, glad that he was already sounding more himself.

Stayne squinted up, eyeing her with disfavor. "I'll tell you what it is, my girl! You are getting above yourself – giving orders to my servants under my nose! If there's one thing I can't abide, it's a managing female!"

Felicity pressed a piece of court

plaster firmly into place over the wound and turned away to rinse out her cloth.

"I can quite see now, sir, why you have never married. You are very nice in your notions of how females should and should not behave. You do not wish them to be clinging and dissolve into tears at the first sharp word, yet neither, it seems, do you wish them to be practical and show initiative."

"Oh-ho! We are sharp-tongued today!" He winced again and put up tentative fingers to his temple. "Am I then so hard to please?"

She shook her head, laughing. "What you require is a paragon, my lord, and they are very hard to come by. You might, of course, take some dutiful little thing and train her to mind your ways. In fact, I wonder you have never done so."

She paused before adding innocently, "I believe Miss Lipscombe to be quite comfortable – though it is a wellknown fact that girls grow to be very like their mothers!"

"Pray come here, Miss Vale."

"No, sir."

"Why not?"

"Because you would box my ears!"

Before the Earl could reply, the door opened to admit a tall, spare man with a kindly, aesthetic face.

"Ah, John," said Felicity. "You may take his lordship away now. It is time he rested. He still looks very pale and undoubtedly has a raging headache."

"Very good, Miss Vale."

John had a great liking for Miss Vale; a young lady of considerable common sense – and always ready with a smile and a pleasant word. He stepped up to the Earl's chair.

"If you would care to take my arm, my lord?"

"No, John – I would not!" said Lord Stayne with dangerous calm. "I shall remain here. I already feel very much improved, thanks to Miss Vale's ministrations! You may bring the brandy."

His valet was not happy; he looked to Felicity, who seemed not the least surprised. She stepped across to feel the

Earl's pulse and found it already much steadier.

"If his lordship prefers to stay here and drink brandy," she said, "I can see no great harm in it."

"Thank you, Miss Vale!" said the Earl with heavy irony.

"Think nothing of it, sir. The brandy will undoubtedly make your head much worse, but it is not within my power to order your life."

"No – I thank God!" he ejaculated. "It moves me profoundly to hear you admit it!"

His jibe flicked her on the raw; she would have snatched her hand away, but his free one caught and held it.

"Such a capable member," he murmured, and his eyes lifted to her face. "I am grateful, in spite of a great many things I may have said to the contrary."

"Oh well . . . as to that, most of them were justified," she acknowledged with an uncertain grin. "I, too, said a great many things . . . I fear I lost my temper."

His expression was inscrutable. "We

223

both lost our tempers," he said abruptly. "It is best forgotten."

"You are very generous, sir." She felt absurdly close to tears. She tried to withdraw her hand and after a moment he released it.

At the door, he called her name. "Tell me – was it really concern for my skin which moved you to abscond with my grays?"

"Of course, my lord." Felicity hesitated, then added, with a rueful twinkle, "but I am bound to confess I had been longing to drive them for an age!"

She wasn't sure if she imagined the laugh which followed on the closing of the door.

After two weeks of frantic activity the school reopened, and Amaryllis finally left for London.

She departed in Stayne's carriage with a mountain of baggage, in an unseasonable flurry of snow, to a clamor of goodbyes.

She was to travel as far as Chippenham, where her friends the Barsetts would meet her and take her on to London. When the carriage had disappeared from view, Felicity suddenly realized how much she was going to miss her.

Chapter Ten

"Do you know how some of our more enterprising pupils have been passing their time these past weeks?"

Something in Ester's voice made Felicity glance up from the progress chart she had been compiling. How different Ester was these days; the hollows in her cheeks had filled out and the pale hair, no longer lank, had been coaxed into soft, shining waves. She had grown into a handsome woman and as though aware of the fact, she moved with a new briskness and confidence.

Her glance moved on to where Willie stood stolidly before a bright Bible painting on the wall. Poor isolated Willie! What really went on behind that blank facade? There were times when she despaired of ever penetrating it fully. Jennie, by contrast, was now a sturdy, lively toddler.

"They have been conducting their own classes," Ester's voice drew her attention back with a jerk. "In that old drover's hut upon the common."

"No! Really?" Felicity sat back with a grin of pure pride. "That's quite a compliment, don't you think?"

"It depends how you look at it," said Ester dryly. She gave Felicity an enigmatic look. "Ask yourself who would most wish to profit from such clandestine tuition?"

"Oh glory! The Manor Court children?"

"Precisely. I only heard about it myself this morning. Our brats have been selling their services at a halfpenny a session, with Lanny Price as their ringleader. He organized the scheme the moment he was off his sickbed."

Felicity smiled ruefully. "I wish he would devote as much energy to his own studies."

"Well, the money's been rolling in from all accounts – with or without parental connivance." Ester stood for a

227

moment in frowning silence, a pile of books in her arms. "The Captain won't like it."

"Need he know?"

"He'll know."

"He's been very quiet lately. Perhaps Lord Stayne's words went home and he has decided to accept the situation."

Felicity's words lacked conviction; they both knew that silence from that quarter was as ominous as the quiet before a storm.

Furthermore, whether Captain Hardman heard about it or not, it was inevitable that the Earl must. He always did. She had a feeling that it was something she was going to find difficult to explain away, which was a pity just when they had begun to establish a certain rapport.

Without Amaryllis to chatter inanities, the dinner table had become a place for intelligent conversation, which sometimes spilled over into arguments lasting well into the evening.

Indeed, they were so comfortable together that she found herself indulging in daydreams of a most dangerous nature. Even so, it was something of a relief when the Earl strode into the breakfast room one morning and laid a letter before her.

Her appetite gone, she pushed away her plate and read swiftly, very much aware of his set face. Captain Hardman certainly hadn't minced matters; phrases such as "gross interference," "incitement to sedition," and "flagrant disregard" leapt at her from the page.

"Oh, really! How absurd!"

"Then there is no truth in his accusation?" queried the Earl grimly.

Felicity hedged, recruiting her defenses with a sip of tea. "A few children getting together to share knowledge – is that so wrong?"

"Don't equivocate. Money changed hands, did it not?"

"Halfpennies, my lord," she pleaded. "It was a childish prank and it won't occur again, I promise you. I have spoken to them most severely."

"So I should hope. I have given Captain Hardman my personal assurances to that effect."

"Oh, thank you." She smiled sunnily at him. "I daresay you have already breakfasted, but will you take a cup of tea, my lord?"

She deduced from his expression that he would not. He said, with a strong degree of exasperation, "You take it very calmly, too calmly. If Hardman were not so bedeviled by trouble among his foundry workers as to have his mind fully occupied, you and your brood might have fared much worse."

"I don't see what he could have done, other than complain," she reasoned. "And I'm not a bit surprised that his foundry workers are in revolt. The man is a petty little tyrant; he will be well served if he comes to a tyrant's end. Fancy picking on children!"

Stayne had been mending the fire with one of the apple logs that stood in the hearth. As the sparks flew up he turned,

230

his exasperation tinged with reluctant laughter.

"You are like a broody hen with those abominable brats! It's woe betide anyone who threatens them!"

"If I am, it's because I am proud of them. They are such good children on the whole, and you must admit they have come on! My only failure seems to be Lanny Price. He still plays truant more often than he attends."

"My dear girl, you are wasting your time there. Lanny Price is a scamp – almost as wily a poacher as his father!"

"Yes, but he does have ability, if one could only channel it," she enthused, selecting a peach from the fruit dish and beginning to peel it. "It was he, you know, who organized those classes upon the common."

"That in no way commends him to me!"

She grinned. "Perhaps not. But you must admit it shows initiative. Of course," she ventured, "they do say that ex-poachers make the best gamekeepers, do they not?"

His look demolished her. "You may take me for a flat, Miss Felicity Vale, but you've windmills in your head if you think I'll swallow bait of that kind!"

"It was just a thought."

The Earl came and stood by her chair, bringing her firmly to her feet.

"And a thought is all it will ever be." With a kind of urgency, he added: "Don't let that crusading zeal of yours blind you to reality, my dear. Lanny Price will never change – but he will break your heart, if you let him!"

The interview left the Earl in a mood of restless dissatisfaction – a mood he was experiencing more often of late and seemed unable to define. It led him now to seek out his head keeper and castigate him for allowing the vermin too much license.

"We are losing far too many of the young chicks to predators. And the rabbit population is becoming a menace!"

Perkins, well used to his lordship's odd quirks of temper, turned a shade

232

ruddier in complexion, shuffled his feet, and agreed stolidly that it was so. He would set more traps and organize a party of guns to deal with the rabbits.

"I'll come out with you now," said the Earl abruptly. "In a couple of hours we should be able to dispose of a satisfactory number."

Perkins mentally consigned his peremptory employer to the devil and reluctantly set aside the thousand and one more urgent jobs he had intended to tackle.

Rather less than two hours they were turning for home, having accounted for more than a score of rabbits and with exacerbated feelings on both sides slightly mollified.

A rustling in the bushes to their left brought them to a halt. His lordship, quicker in his reactions, fired first; there was a squeal more human than animal. The Earl thrust his gun at Perkins and covered the space in a few urgent strides. The spaniels were there before him, sniffing curiously.

Lanny Price lay face down, his head turned to one side, his features twisted in a silent mask of agony and his eyes wide with fear. The back of his threadbare smock was peppered with blood-smeared pellet holes. Near his outflung hand lay a dead pigeon.

"How about that, now!" said Perkins, peering over the Earl's shoulder. "It appears we've caught ourselves something more'n rabbits, m'lord. That's what I call a good morning's work!"

Stayne made no answer. He was totally confounded by the helpless anger coursing through him. Why? Oh why the devil must it be the Price boy!

"You very nearly got yourself killed this time," he said roughly.

"Well, he'll take no more from this patch – or any other, for that matter." The keeper stooped to hoist Lanny to his feet. "Just you leave him to me, m'lord. I'll keep him safe under lock and key until you're ready to deal with him."

"No!" The Earl's voice grated. He knew Perkins was looking at him oddly –

probably thought he had taken leave of his senses! Could be he was right, at that. He heard himself saying: "No. I'll carry the boy. You cut along and get Dr. Belvedere. Take him to the Price cottage."

The keeper opened his mouth – and thought better of it. You didn't cross the Earl when he wore that look!

Stayne lifted the slight, unyielding body and was appalled by its lack of flesh. The boy was no more than a weightless bag of bones.

The children had been in perverse moods all morning. Both Felicity and Ester had been obliged to rebuke them on more than one occasion. When Felicity saw several of them peering through the window and whispering, her voice grew uncommonly sharp.

"Sit down this instant and get on with your work! The next child to incur a rebuke will be punished."

Reluctantly the heads were drawn back, but Lanny's younger sister, Meg, put up a tentative hand, her face paler than usual.

"Please, miss, it's our Lanny. 'Is lord-ship's gone past carrying 'im . . . 'e looks bad, miss!"

Felicity arrived at the Price cottage in time to hear Stayne's voice banked with suppressed fury.

" . . . in God's name, woman! Is one fool in the family not enough? Get it into that boy's head, will you, that poaching is a deadly business! And I do mean deadly. He would be dead at this moment had I been using ball instead of shot. He will not be so lucky a second time!" Felicity saw him take out a coin. "Get some food into these children. Mind me, now – if your man robs you of that money, he will answer to me!"

Stayne came sweeping through the doorway, almost knocking Felicity down. There was a curious blindness in his face. When she spoke, he grasped her arm most cruelly.

"So much for your protégé, madam! I warned you, did I not? If you cannot

236

make him mind you better, the only future he will enjoy is a free passage to Botany Bay!"

He was gone and she was left staring into the pitifully bare room where two toddlers played in the straw, unaware of the drama being enacted. Lanny lay on a rough palliasse in one corner, white-faced but stoically silent.

When Felicity went across to speak to him, he turned his face to the wall. His mother stood, still clutching the precious coin, her youngest child in her arms and an expression of bitter hopelessness in her eyes which moved Felicity almost to tears.

Perkins arrived with the doctor, and left again at once, stiff with disapproval. Felicity ran after him to find out what had happened. His account, though reluctantly given, was picturesque.

"Oh, poor Lanny! He might have been killed!"

"Not that one, Miss Vale, though it 'ud have been no more'n he deserved. It'll take a while to dig the shot out of him, and he'll not sit down for a spell, but he'll live to hang, and so I would have told his lordship, but he took it uncommon strange when I ventured to suggest that he should make an example of the boy."

Perkins rubbed his rather bulbous nose, perplexed and none too pleased at having to let a known poacher, caught in the act, slip through his fingers.

The accident distressed Felicity; it obsessed her mind for the remainder of the day. By evening she had little appetite, nor did she relish the prospect of meeting Lord Stayne in his present frame of mind. This much at least she was spared; Lord Stayne did not come to dinner.

An attempt to quiz Cavanah elicited only that his lordship was a trifle indisposed, yet she had the distinct impression that he was being evasive.

Crossing the Long Gallery later, she met John. His lordship's valet carried a bottle of brandy. He bade her good evening as he paused by the door of a small salon. When she asked after Lord

Stayne, the man hesitated.

"His lordship is . . . not quite himself this evening, Miss Vale," he said, and his kindly face wore the same blank look Cavanah's had done.

Felicity looked from him to the bottle and her eyes widened in sudden comprehension. "You cannot mean . . . is he foxed, John?"

"Jug-bitten, miss," admitted the unhappy valet.

"Goodness! But does he . . . is he in the habit of . . .?"

"Oh, no! Hardly ever, miss. I disremember the last time he was castaway . . . no, I tell a lie . . . it was the time we heard that Master Antony had been killed."

"Then why now? Not because of what happened this morning, surely?" She had no doubt but that everyone knew of the events of the morning.

"It's not for me to say, Miss Vale, but he's been acting uncommonly strange ever since. It isn't like him."

"No." Felicity was puzzled. "John, let

me take the tray in."

"I wouldn't recommend it, miss. Got an uncertain turn of temper has his lordship when he's foxed."

She laughed. "That's all right. I have dealt with soldiers in all stages of drunkenness. I doubt his lordship will have the power to shock me."

John's mouth pursed in lines of disapproval, but he surrendered the tray and opened the door for her.

She had never been in the room before. It was quite charming; small by Cheynings standards and much given over to crimson velvet and rosewood furniture, with a pair of comfortable looking plush armchairs set beside a blazing fire.

In one of these sprawled Lord Stayne, coatless, his long legs stretched into the hearth. The candlelight fell on a riot of silver hair, more disheveled than fashion could ever demand. His cravat had been tugged loose and an empty brandy glass dangled from limp fingers.

He was staring fixedly into the fire and

did not immediately perceive her.

"You've been an interminable time over that bottle, curse you," he growled, and then, as though sensing a change in the atmosphere, his glittering, unblinking stare shifted to Felicity; its intensity sent little ripples of shock through her.

In contrast, his voice, though harsh, was uncaring. "Who gave you leave to come in here?"

"No one, my lord," she said as calmly as she was able.

"I see," he sneered. "This is more of your damned officiousness, is it? Well, I am in no mood for your homilies tonight, so you may hand over my bottle and get out!"

Felicity put the bottle on the table beside him, distressed to see him less than himself.

"Lanny isn't badly hurt," she ventured. "He is in some pain and his pride will smart, but he should not have been where he was, so you must not blame yourself."

The Earl laughed a little wildly and

poured a generous measure of brandy with an unsteady hand, jarring the bottle against the rim of the glass.

"Thank you. But I don't blame myself, my dear Miss Vale." He saluted her mockingly and drank. "I blame you."

"Me?" Felicity stood rooted to the spot.

"Yes. You." He nodded. "Because of you, I have been sitting here with my life set out before me. It might surprise you to know that I have always considered myself a just man – giving praise where it is due, and rigorously punishing the wrongdoer, but always fair, mind you – a magistrate should always strive to be fair."

"My lord, please . . ."

"And then you came along, Felicity Vale, with your uncompromising ways and outspokenness and your . . . shining honesty! And what has happened? I'll tell you what has happened!" He leveled his glass at her and a little of the brandy slopped over the rim. "You've given me a cursed social conscience,

242

madam – and it don't sit well!"

There was a tight lump in Felicity's throat. "Sir – you are not yourself..."

"Ha! Don't boggle at plain speaking now, my girl! I am as drunk as a wheelbarrow! I strongly recommend it for inducing clarity of mind!" He leaned forward confidentially. "I know that had I shot that boy twelve months back – killed him, even – I wouldn't have turned a hair. Child or no, he is a known poacher – a wrongdoer if ever there was one!

"Yet today, when I picked him up, he was just a boy like Jamie – a boy, appallingly undersized with the bones sticking out of him; a boy with none of Jamie's advantages... yet game as a pebble for all that!"

The bottle clinked against the glass again. "The realization had a profound effect on me. As a consequence, my head keeper thinks I've gone soft in the upper works – and who's to say he's not right – because I won't prosecute!"

He rested his head against the chair as

though exhausted by the long and rather rambling disclosure.

"Now for God's sake, leave me!"

Felicity was suddenly very angry. "That I will not!" she cried. "How dare you so belittle yourself! All because of some silly accident. Why, I had by far rather you turned violent and took to throwing things! It would become you better than this maudlin self-indulgence!"

"Would it?" Stayne came to his feet with surprising agility for a man three parts disguised. He seized her wrist and jerked her forward until she lay helpless against his chest. His other hand forced her chin upward and she found his eyes heart-stoppingly close, blazing into her own. "Is this violent enough for you?"

She saw quite clearly the faint mark on his temple from the injury she had treated – and the fast-beating pulse close beside it. And then, in a haze of brandy fumes, his mouth came down on hers, hard and demanding, blotting everything out and setting the room spinning . . .

As abruptly as he had possessed her, he let her go, almost pushing her from him.

Felicity grabbed a nearby chair for support, the blood pounding through her veins, while the Earl stood hunched over the fire, one arm resting along the mantelshelf.

"So much for violence!" The harsh voice shook slightly. "Forgive me. I must disgust you!"

"No, sir."

He uttered a short, derisive laugh. "Then you are more generous than I deserve. I disgust myself! You had better go."

Felicity hesitated. "I cannot go, leaving you like this."

He looked up, disbelieving at first – then he put back his head and laughed. She eyed him anxiously; the wildness had gone, though his eyes were still over-bright.

"What an indomitable girl you are!"

he gasped. "To what lengths would you go, I wonder, if you deemed it your duty to save me from myself?"

She smiled uncertainly.

"Oh, go along, girl. I am no longer out of my senses, I promise you! And accept my humble apologies, I usually hold my liquor rather better!"

Felicity slept not a wink that night. Her own senses were in a turmoil, hovering between wild elation and depression; in the first pale light of dawn she finally gave a name to the pangs that assailed her – it was love, total and irrevocable!

She wondered if Stayne would be at breakfast, and if so, could she face him with composure? In the event, all her heart-searching availed her little.

"His lordship left for London at first light, Miss Vale," said Cavanah. "He will be joining Mrs. Delamere there, no doubt."

Chapter Eleven

"It's Mamma! It's Mamma! And there are gentlemen with her!" Jamie scrambled down from the windowseat in the nursery and rushed toward the door. Mr. Burnett's quiet voice halted him and desired him to come back and tidy his toys away first.

The instant, if reluctant, obedience to this command brought a smile to Felicity's lips; in the few short months that Aloysius Burnett had been with them, Jamie was already much steadier.

While she waited for Jamie, she wandered across to the window. The nursery was high up in the West Wing, and through the rain-drenched panes the view was blurred.

There were two post chaises drawn up and several hacks were being led away. Nearby, a group of gentlemen stood in a huddle, swathed in long, enveloping cloaks, with rain dripping from the brims of their beaver hats. Even with the distorted view, however, she was certain that none stood tall enough to be Lord Stayne. She reproved herself for the stab of disappointment.

The house had suddenly come to life. The hall was full of people; they stood around the two fires, shedding wet clothes, all laughing and talking at once.

Amaryllis was radiant; she wore a dress in her favorite deep blue, and an extremely modish poke bonnet of Gros de Naples, with matching ribbons. This she threw carelessly onto a chair and, with a pale, lacy wrap slipping from her shoulders, held out her arms to Jamie, smothering him in kisses until he wriggled free, scarlet with embarrassment. She made a little moue and declared that he had grown beyond everything and that her baby was gone forever!

Then Amaryllis turned her brilliant blue eyes on Felicity.

"Fliss! You are looking a trifle worn.

Who can wonder at it, buried here all alone . . . and with this incessant rain! Everyone complains of it . . . no one can remember a worse summer! The Colchesters, who have recently returned from the Continent, found the weather even worse there, with snow and hailstones and the crops all destroyed!"

Jamie had been watching the procession of baggage and tugged at his mother's arm. "Did you bring me a present?"

Felicity reproved him, but Amaryllis only laughed. "Yes, darling – lots. Oh, Fliss, just wait until you see all I have brought from Town! Silks and brocades, cambrics and Indian muslins from Layton and Shears in Henrietta Street . . . Oh, and a pale yellow crepe that I am determined was just made for you! Now that I am back, I mean to take you in hand, my dear . . . I have silk stockings and French gloves and . . . oh, so many things."

"Lord Stayne did not travel back with you?" Felicity despised herself for asking and was well served when Amaryllis laughed casually.

"Good gracious, no! We have scarce seen him! He came once to Almacks, but he stayed only long enough to stand up with me and once with Lucinda, which puffed her mother up no end!"

"But I have brought Uncle Perry," she continued. "The Barsetts have come, too, and Francis and Lydia Spencer and the Honeysetts . . . and there is someone else, too."

Amaryllis beckoned and a fair, slightly built young man detached himself from one of the groups near the fire. There was something vaguely familiar about his easy stride and splendid military side-whiskers.

"Well now, young Felicity Vale!" he said with a grin.

She grasped the outstretched hand with a cry of pleasure. "Major Tremaine! How very nice!"

"Haven't I been clever?" said Amaryllis.

"I've known this young lady since she was so high."

"I used to sew on all your buttons," laughed Felicity. Her eyes had gone instinctively to the empty sleeve pinned to his chest and her heart gave a lurch of dismay. Johnny Tremaine of all people! The regiment's undisputed Romeo and daredevil.

When Amaryllis left them alone, she touched the sleeve with tentative fingers. "I'm so sorry," she said impulsively. "I didn't know."

"Don't you fret my dear girl," he said cheerfully. "Why, I am already scarcely missing it. Alastair reckons I am becoming insufferably cocksure!"

"How is Colonel Patterson – and Mrs. Patterson?"

"Well enough. They are back in England now. Alastair has secured himself a very comfortable staff appointment . . . at Horse Guards, no less! What it is to have influence!" The jibe was devoid of malice, the two men having been firm friends for many years.

251

"You must give me their direction," said Felicity.

"With pleasure, though Mollie will be writing to you herself, no doubt, as soon as they are settled. They have taken a house near Islington Spa. She will, no doubt, insist upon your visiting them."

"Oh, it will be nice to see them . . . and the children. How they will have grown!"

Felicity could not fail to notice as they talked, how his eye followed Amaryllis. It would have been astonishing, she supposed, if Amaryllis had not taken his eye.

"And what will you do now?" she asked gently.

He shrugged, and the laughing gray eyes looked momentarily bleak.

"I'm still with the regiment, but I shall most likely sell out. I doubt there being any great future for a one-armed man. Besides . . ." He left the sentence unfinished, but his eyes were again on Amaryllis, who was coming toward them with Sir Peregrine and Jamie. "Bye

252

the bye," he said, bringing his attention back with an effort, "I haven't said how sorry I am . . . about your parents. You had left by the time I had the news. It was a wretched business! So many good lives lost."

"Yes," she said simply. "Sometimes I cannot believe it is a whole twelvemonth since . . ."

The others joined them and no more was said. Sir Peregrine kissed Felicity soundly and asked how she did; then the guests dispersed to their hastily prepared rooms and Felicity was called to the kitchen, at Cavanah's urgent behest, to reassure Mrs. Hudson that she was more than equal to the task of conjuring a meal for upward of a dozen people with no more than three hours' notice.

Later in the evening, when Lord and Lady Spencer and the Honeysetts were engaged in a rubber of whist and the rest of the party had gathered around the pianoforte, Sir Peregrine drew Felicity a little to one side.

"I've been observing you, child – sitting there in your pretty green dress. You're looking peaky. Not been having trouble with that oaf, Hardman, again, eh?"

"No," she said quickly – too quickly. She added a bright smile of reassurance. "No, really – I promise you."

"Captain Hardman has been away for a large part of the summer," she told Uncle Perry. "He has been having a lot of trouble at his Shropshire foundries, I believe . . . a meeting organized by Bamford and Hunt which got out of hand. The Militia were called in and it all got rather nasty."

The worry showed in her voice. "But now he is back and in a towering rage to find his barns have been burned."

"What! It hasn't spread this far, surely? We heard rumors of uprisings in Essex and Suffolk . . ."

Sir Peregrine's voice carried above the conversation. The whist players paused in their play and the pianoforte trailed off on a discord.

"There hasn't been trouble here – on

Stayne's land?" cried Amaryllis.

"No, no. Only Manor Court farm has suffered so far."

"Oh – that man!" Amaryllis shrugged and instantly lost interest.

Felicity kept to herself the fear that the burning of the Captain's barns was not part of the general unrest, but the work of a few local troublemakers taking advantage of an already tense situation. Her fear was heightened by a disquieting suspicion that some of her older boys might have become involved.

"It is a wonder that anything will burn in all this rain," observed Lizzie Barsett with an out-of-place levity which earned her a quelling frown from her brother.

Tom Barsett, unlike his pretty, dizzy sister, was a stolid, earnest young man. He took his stance rather pompously near the fireplace.

"We have a friend in Cambridgeshire whose farm was attacked not two weeks since – his ricks all but destroyed!"

Lady Spencer dropped her cards with a little cry.

"Well, I think it is quite dweadful," she complained with a delicate shudder. "The labowing classes are getting out of hand!"

Felicity was aware of a rising anger which she fought hard to contain. "Perhaps that is because some of them are close to starvation," she explained in a tight voice. "The enclosures deprived them of the strips of land where they used to grow a little food, and keep a cow or a pig or two of their own! Now the prices are soaring. They cannot even afford bread! There were near-riots at the bakery in Stapleforth two days ago."

The atmosphere in the elegant blue and rose drawing room had become charged; Amaryllis was making frantic gestures to Felicity to let the matter drop, but Lord Francis now entered the lists. He was highly displeased to find his game ruined. Furthermore, he resented being preached at by a slip of a girl, who was ill-qualified as he saw it to judge any but the most parochial issues . . . and who seemed possessed of the most reactionary views!

"Prices are hitting at everyone, ma'am," he said in hectoring tones, his face ruddier than usual. "The banks are calling in their money all over the country. Your peasants are not the only sufferers, I assure you!"

"No, but they are least able to bear the brunt."

"Don't you believe it, m'dear!" Sir Peregrine was now on ground he knew well. "It's my opinion that ruin strikes every bit as hard when you're plump in the pocket – more so, in fact. Why, d'ye know, the Gazette last week was full of bankruptcies! Some of them came as a shock to me, I can tell you."

Lizzie giggled nervously. "Even Mr. Brummell has been obliged to flee the country."

"Ah, poor George! Things won't be the same without him."

Johnny Tremaine was quietly picking out a tune with one finger on the keyboard of the pianoforte. "Left a mountain of debts behind him, so I heard."

"I saw him at Almacks once," said Amaryllis, relieved that the conversation had taken a more comfortable turn. "I'm sure I couldn't see anything very special about him. He wasn't half so fine as some."

"Then you lack discernment, puss, if you'll forgive me for saying so." Sir Peregrine took out a very prettily enameled gold snuffbox and offered it around before taking a liberal pinch himself. "Do you recall how he was in his prime, Francis?"

"By Jericho, yes!"

"I mind being at dinner with him," chuckled Sir Peregrine, now firmly launched into reminiscent vein. "He'd his manservant behind his chair to tell him who was either side of him. That way the Beau was able to converse quite prettily with his neighbors without the slightest danger to the folds of his cravat."

The anecdote was greeted with delighted laughter and the tensions eased.

Felicity looked around the room and

258

despaired. These well-fed, well-dressed, and, on the whole, harmless paragons of society filled her with a sense of helplessness. How could they even begin to comprehend? Had any one of them, she wondered, the least conception of the kind of poverty – the gnawing hunger which drives men to violence?

She had come pretty close a few times, and so probably had Johnny Tremaine, but at least an army on the march could forage and, if necessary, commandeer food.

Uncle Perry patted her hand. "Your feelings do you credit, child," he murmured with uncanny perception. "But don't despair of us completely, I beg you! Human beings, are by nature, selfish, but give us time, m'dear ... give us time. All will be set to rights in time, you'll see."

She did see – and smiled a little bleakly, wondering if he realized just how quickly time would run out for some!

A few miles away in the woods of Manor

Court, two figures, a man and a boy, moved with practiced stealth, melting into the deepest shadows. The night-black woods held no secrets for these two; their eyes were trained to see as well as any wild cat's, so that no stirring of life, however infinitesimal, escaped them.

Lanny hadn't wanted to come, but his pa had talked him around.

"Anything you take yourself, lad, you can keep to take home to your ma. Just so long as you helps me with me traps."

With things the way they were, the temptation had been too much. But he hadn't told Ma ... she'd made him promise not to go out any more and he felt bad about breaking his word. It wasn't as though he got a thrill from it, even ... not the way he used to, though he'd rather die than admit it!

Miss Vale ... she wouldn't like it, either. She hadn't 'xactly made him promise ... not the way Ma had ... She said you had to do things right for the right reasons ... not just to please other

260

folk. He'd been going to school pretty regular since that "other business" ... even begun to enjoy it, though you wouldn't catch him admitting that, either!

Still ... she was all right, was Miss Vale. He got a queer lump in his throat thinking how disappointed she'd be ... not angry ... that wouldn't be so bad ... just disappointed ... and kind of quiet...

"Hold hard, lad!" Dick Price laid a warning hand on his son's arm. There were sounds – voices – coming nearer. They passed by uncomfortably close – several big dark shapes – and snatches of conversation drifted across to where they stood.

" ... in a regular taking, 'e was! Fair spoilin' for a fight...."

" ... cold, flamin' rage ... you know how 'e can be! Said it was time some folk learned ... this time he'd handle it his-self ..."

" ... wants to watch it! That Stayne's no looby ... More ways to skin a cat . . ." The voices were fading.

"Wait here," Lanny's pa hissed. "I'm going to follow 'em. I want to hear more."

He was gone with no more than a whisper of sound. Lanny waited, fidgeting a little as time passed. A melancholy owl hooted and presently a hedgehog came snuffling through the undergrowth searching for grubs. It curled into a spiky ball as Lanny picked it up and stuffed it into his pocket. Ma'd need more than one miserable little hedgehog to make her overlook his broken promise, but it was a start.

When the scream came, it reverberated through the darkness, shattering the still night. Lanny was sweating as he ran, slipping on the damp mossy earth and knowing before he got there what he must find. The capricious moon, coming from behind a cloud, shed a cold, dispassionate light through the motionless trees.

His pa lay staring in horror at the bloody pulped remains of what moments before had been his leg, now locked fast in the teeth of a man trap. His gasping sobs seemed scarcely human, and Lanny stood petrified with terror until a sense of urgency overtook him.

He sank to his knees, tearing with hopeless, inadequate fingers at the jaws of the trap, his own fierce sobs mingling with his pa's.

"You're ... wasting time ... boy. You'll not ... budge it."

Footsteps were crashing through the undergrowth and there was a lot of shouting.

Dick Price roused himself from the welcoming blackness of oblivion. His voice rasped. "Get out. Can't you see ... I'm done for ..."

"Over here!" came an exultant cry. "This way."

"For the love of God! Go, boy ... while you can ... tell your ma ... sorry. Now go." He reared up agonizedly and gave Lanny a push. The boy went sprawling, scrambled up, and stared at his pa with a last, mute appeal. As if on cue, the moon vanished, and with a despairing cry Lanny plunged off into the trees, running like a wild animal – and above the sobbing that was his own breathing, he imagined a sound like the crack of a gunshot.

Chapter Twelve

Dick Price's body was found washed up on the riverbank where Lord Stayne's land met the parish boundary. In the Earl's absence the magistrate from the adjoining parish was notified. Sir Geoffrey Blunt received the news with undisguised satisfaction; the manner of the notorious poacher's demise was of little interest to him.

When Felicity protested to him that Dick Price had been most foully murdered, he had shrugged and expressed it as his opinion that someone had saved the hangman a job. Feelings were running very high in the district where poaching was concerned.

Did Miss Vale not know, he said, that the law now only required two magistrates sitting together to pass sentence? Why only last week, Mr. Partridge, from

Barns Hollow, and himself had dealt very summarily with some eight or nine of the varmints. The three who had been apprehended in a pitched battle with gamekeepers had been executed and the remainder, caught on private land with the tools of their trade, so to speak, were to be transported at His Majesty's pleasure.

No, indeed, Miss Vale need not trouble her head over the manner in which one such rogue may have met his end!

Oh, how Felicity longed for Lord Stayne! Perhaps there was little, if anything, he could have done, but at least he would have acted with more humanity!

And then there was the worry of Lanny; he hadn't been seen since the night his father died. His mother had turned up on the school doorstep two days later, gaunt with worry.

"I'm that sorry to trouble you, miss," she began. "But I know as you've alus had a soft spot for our Lanny . . . and I'm that afeared!"

Felicity assured her that it was no trouble.

"With my man it was different . . . I reckon I alus knew it would end that way, but the boy . . ." Her mouth started to tremble and Felicity made her come in and sit down. The poor woman was near to breaking. "I know as he went with 'is pa, miss . . . though he swore he wouldn't ever again. Dick had a way of talkin' him 'round . . . only why hasn't he come home?"

"Perhaps he is frightened . . . or even ashamed?"

"No, Miss Vale. Our Lanny's no coward, whatever else 'e may be," asserted his mother stubbornly, and Felicity was bound to agree. "I wouldn't worry so, only I know as it was Manor Court they went to, and that Captain Hardman'd stop at nothing!"

"How can you be sure? Your husband was found a long way from there, you know."

"It was Manor Court, miss."

Her certainty, together with Lanny's

continuing absence, gnawed at Felicity, making her less appreciative than she should have been of her cousin's generosity. True to her word, Amaryllis had come home laden with bolts of silks and muslins and crepes, with bonnets and fur tippets, ribbons and laces, and all manner of fripperies . . . and she plied Felicity with gifts until she cried, "Enough!"

"Nonsense!" cried Amaryllis. She spilled a cascade of enticing color onto Felicity's bed and marched across to fling open the cupboard door.

"I declare, I have never seen such a spartan closet!" she exclaimed with brutal candor. "Why, there cannot be above five or six dresses, aside from your blacks, which you cannot wish ever to don again!"

"Six dresses are ample for my needs," protested Felicity, half laughing.

"Then you shall have six new ones – no, no – I insist! It shall be my way of repaying you for the marvelous time I had in London, which I should never have had without your intervention. Besides," she added ingenuously, "I have brought back so much, I shall scarcely miss these few lengths!"

"Oh! But I hardly think his lordship intended you to be spending his money on dresses for me." Felicity frowned and began to gather up the tumbled material. "Indeed, I am persuaded that I should not accept."

"Fiddle! As if that signified! I am determined you shall have your dresses. And furthermore, Ester shall help you to make up the yellow crepe at once, for I intend to hold a ball."

Felicity gave up the argument without too many qualms. She looked curiously at her cousin.

"Amaryllis? How well do you like Johnny Tremaine?"

"Goodness! What a question!" Amaryllis feigned nonchalance, but she colored up very prettily, none the less. "He is well enough, I suppose, though I think him a shocking flirt!"

"He used to be, certainly, but I have a feeling he may be ready to reform."

Felicity hesitated, well aware of her cousin's aversion to illness in any form and unsure how far it extended. She would not have Johnny hurt any further. "His . . . disability does not offend you?"

"Of course not!" Amaryllis protested. "And anyway, I cannot see what that has to do with anything. You are asking far too many questions." She whisked from the room before she could be further interrogated.

Felicity had never seen beyond the boundary wall of Manor Court. Now she drove her gig smartly up the front drive, her straight-backed confidence hiding an inner quaking. It had taken every ounce of courage she possessed to come, her fears for Lanny's safety having finally grown beyond what was bearable.

The wheels crunched on the wide semicircle of gravel in front of the house. Manor Court was modest in size when compared to Cheynings; a square arcadian manor house much as its name suggested, pleasantly grown over with creeper.

As she halted the gig at the front steps, two men came as if from nowhere. One of them, the big Negro, reached out a huge black paw to grasp the gelding's harness, while his companion slouched over to Felicity and leaned close, his hairy arms spread out along the side of the gig, barring her way.

"I wish to see Captain Hardman," she informed him crisply, clasping her hands very tight and praying that they would not disgrace her by shaking.

"Do you now?" His eyes moved insolently over her. "But will the Capt'n want to see you, think you?"

Felicity stiffened angrily. "Perhaps you would be good enough to ask him?"

The man shrugged, spat reflectively into a nearby flower bed, and ambled off to inquire.

She was presently ushered into a pleasant, chintzy parlor, not in the least suited to its owner.

"Miss Vale?" The Captain sat at a desk with his back to the window. He made no effort to rise, nor did he ask her to be seated. "I am extremely busy. Be good enough to state the purpose of your visit."

The light voice had a nervy edge which hadn't been there before, as though, Felicity thought, his problems were beginning to get on top of him.

"It concerns the murdered poacher."

A tiny muscle at the corner of his mouth twitched at her choice of word. "What is that scoundrel to me? He was found on Stayne's land."

Felicity could feel her palms growing damp as her eyes met his pale, empty ones. "But he did not die there, did he? Stayne does not use those abominable man traps; everyone knows it. No – he died here on your land, Captain Hardman – trapped and then shot by your men, with or without your connivance."

A small, dagger-like knife lay on the desk. He picked it up and began to tap it twitchily against the desk edge.

"You are too looose-tongued by far, miss! I trust you are not spreading these vicious theories of yours about the village?"

"I don't need to, sir. People know well enough how Dick Price met his end; they just don't care very much. And though I care, my concern at present is for his son."

"The red-haired brat? Where does he come in? You are talking in riddles, ma'am."

"I believe Lanny was out with his father that night."

"And so?" The knife stilled. Reluctantly, Felicity was forced to admit that his perplexity seemed genuine.

"Nobody has seen him since," she said, less surely.

A thin smile failed to reach his eyes. "And you imagine that I have him chained up in my cellar, perhaps? You are welcome to search where you please. I will call Rayner."

"No," Felicity said quickly, convinced that he would not suggest it if

273

there was the least hope of her finding Lanny. "No, that will not be necessary. I am sorry to have troubled you, sir." She felt sick with despair as she turned to the door.

Captain Hardman saw something of that despair mirrored in her face. He flung down the knife and stood up. "One moment, madam."

He strutted across to the fireplace and pulled on a silken bell rope, and then stood with his back to the fire, his legs aggressively straddling the hearth.

"You have the accursed effrontery to invade the privacy of my home, accusing me of God knows what infamy! You spread scurrilous rumors which strike at my integrity... encourage insubordination... I would not even put it past you to have been actively concerned in the recent attacks upon my property."

"No. You have no grounds!"

"Grounds enough, madam! As much as you have for your vile insinuations!"

The door opened and the hairy man came in.

"If you were a man, I could demand satisfaction," the Captain continued inexorably. "I might even be considered justified in taking a horsewhip to you." He paused significantly. "But how does one deal with an obstinate, trouble-making schoolmarm? It seems I must needs devise some appropriate means of alleviating my grievance and impressing upon you the ... impropriety of visiting a gentleman's house unattended! You are unattended?"

The inference and the menacing presence of the man at her back made Felicity's flesh crawl, but she said steadily, "I am, sir. But you should know that I left a note with a maid. If I am not back within –" she glanced at an ornate French clock on the mantelshelf above his head "– fifteen minutes from now, she is to take it at once to Sir Peregrine Trent. You will remember Sir Peregrine, I think?"

She watched the color creep up under

his skin. There was an uncomfortable moment when she wasn't sure what would happen. When he spoke, his voice was clipped with fury and overlaid with a curious emphasis.

"Miss Vale is leaving, Rayner. It appears that, for the moment, we are unable to extend to her our intended hospitality. Perhaps we shall be afforded the opportunity at a later date."

"I doubt it," Felicity said shortly.

"Who knows, ma'am?" the high, light voice concluded. "You are an impetuous young woman! You might have spared yourself this interview had you stopped to think. Did it ever occur to you that, had I apprehended the poacher's brat on my land, he would have been instantly handed over to Sir Geoffrey Blunt? Now, there is a magistrate who dispenses my kind of justice!"

Felicity was never so glad to escape into the fresh air. She longed to spring the gelding, but pride prevailed and her retreat was as calm and ordered as her arrival had been. Only when she reached the road did she relax, to find that her back was drenched in perspiration.

The preparations for the ball had gone ahead with enthusiasm; in the end, more than seventy people were certain to attend. Amaryllis had engaged musicians all the way from Bath, there being none nearer worthy of her attention. For days beforehand all was in a bustle; the ballroom, an extraordinary brainchild of the 8th Earl, so reminiscent of the Regent's Pavilion at Brighton with its domed roof and exotic interior, had not been in use since the late Countess's day, and though it had received routine attention, it was now found to require much refurbishing before it met with Amaryllis's satisfaction.

There was to be a buffet laid out in the dining room and one of the smaller salons had been designated as a card room.

The final preparations were at their chaotic peak when, unexpected as ever, Lord Stayne walked in on them. He

surveyed the scene in an ominous silence, demanded to know what the devil
was going on, and without waiting for
answer, added a rider to the effect that he
had obviously returned to a madhouse!

But by evening he appeared to have
accepted the inescapable with at least
tolerably good grace. He stood in the
doorway of the drawing room prior to
dinner; among the glittering array of
guests already assembled Felicity
thought him by far the most distingu-
ished. His gray hair had been pomaded
to a gleaming silver, making his eyebrows look very black in contrast. He
was formally dressed in a black long-tail-
ed coat, white satin waistcoat, and knee-
breeches; in the folds of his cravat a dia-
mond winked.

His glance traveled slowly around the
room, passed her by, and then slowly returned. His eyes widened a little and he
inclined his head. Felicity's heart, which
had already risen into her throat to suf-
focate her, now gave a treacherous lurch;
she took herself firmly in hand and smil-

278

ed back, knowing that she looked her best.

The pale yellow crepe had turned out well; she had resisted all persuasion by Amaryllis to deck it with frills and furbelows.

"No, no, my dear," she had protested, laughing. "You must see that I was not built for frills! Believe me, I should resemble nothing so much as one of Mrs. Hudson's great lemon blancmanges, festooned in whipped cream!"

Instead she had kept the lines simple and flowing, edging the dress down the front with a double row of cream lace; worn over a slip of cream satin, the result was more than she had hoped for. A fine gilt comb, another of her cousin's gifts, set off her chestnut curls to advantage.

"I scarcely recognized my severely practical schoolmistress," murmured the Earl when he finally reached her side. "I had no idea you were looking to outshine my sister-in-law!"

Although his humor was mocking, there was a slight restraint in his manner; remembering their last encounter, Felicity supposed he must also be remembering. She resolved to show him that he need not regard it.

She said with her normal good-humored raillery, "Thank you, my lord. Such a compliment from you must indeed be accounted an accolade! And one that I shall treasure!"

There was an immediate easing of tension.

"You think I would offer you Spanish coin?" he challenged quizzically.

"Gracious, no!" Felicity feigned shocked surprise. "Other people might empty the butter boat over one quite lavishly and think nothing of it, but that is not your way, my lord! I have too often been the recipient of your... frankness, and am therefore persuaded that you must be sincere!"

Stayne's smile ripened into an appreciative chuckle and Felicity found the oddest things happening to her knees.

Later, a small group formed in one corner of the ballroom.

"Has this madcap laid siege to your horses yet, Lord Stayne?" asked Johnny Tremaine.

"Don't speak of it!" groaned Amaryllis.

Felicity and the Earl exchanged glances.

"It was Johnny who taught me to drive," she explained demurely. "One hot, dusty summer in Lisbon when I was with the Pattersons."

"Ha! You, was it?" observed the Earl pithily. "You've a great deal to answer for, let me tell you, Major!"

Johnny Tremaine laughed. "She was just fifteen at the time, mad about horses, and as persistent a skinny, long brown beanpole as I ever came across! Of course," he grinned, "she's filled out a bit since then, but I've no doubt she's still as stubborn."

Again the glances locked. The Earl lifted a mocking brow. "Since it would be ungallant in me to agree, I shall refrain from comment."

Mrs. Lipscombe watched the laughing group, disapproval in every rigid line of her ample form. Her stiff purple brocade crackled as she turned to her husband.

"I cannot think such free and easy manners becoming in a young woman. Miss Vale does herself no credit by putting herself forward in such a way! As for her dress – I hope I may never see our daughter in such a dress!"

"Not a chance of it, I should say," offered the mouse-quiet Mr. Lipscombe, with an unaccustomed gleam in his eyes as they rested on Felicity. "Lucinda ain't got the figure for it!"

"Horace!" Mrs. Lipscombe's mouth dropped open, but the violent stream of rebuke about to be unleashed against the poor unfortunate man was stayed temporarily by a further burst of laughter. The incensed woman rounded instead upon her daughter who stood at her side, charmingly attired in silver net over white satin.

"Lucinda!" she snapped. "Why do you stand here, allowing yourself to be totally eclipsed? Lord Stayne and Amaryllis must be wishing you to join their little party. I am sure his lordship will think it very strange if you hang back!"

Much later still, when Felicity was leaving the floor, breathless and laughing after an energetic spell of waltzing with Johnny, the Earl came up and determinedly took her arm. Johnny surrendered her with a grin and sauntered away. Stayne led her to a quiet corner of the room when he sat her down and put a glass of cordial in her hand.

Felicity sipped it gratefully. "Thank you, my lord. You can have no idea how much I was needing this."

"You are very popular this evening," he said dryly. "I had almost resigned myself to watching you from afar."

Her eyes twinkled at him over the rim of the glass. "Now that is flummery, my lord – and well you know it!"

"Perhaps. But I came back with so many things I wanted to say to you. I hadn't expected all this." He waved an impatient hand at the ballroom floor where the couples were forming up for a quadrille.

Felicity saw Amaryllis with Johnny, her floating blue silk melting intimately into the darker blue of Johnny's coat as his fair head bent to something she was saying – and her own heart was beating fast.

So many things I wanted to say to you. Stayne's words filled her with hope, for surely he had never looked at her in quite that way before!

"That is a very personable young man."

Felicity's eyes were still following the couple on the ballroom floor, still misty with dreams. She saw that the Earl's glance had taken the same direction.

"Johnny?"

"You know him well, I infer?"

"Oh, yes," she agreed blissfully. "I have known Johnny forever! He was one of Colonel Patterson's most promising young officers, always about the place." Felicity laughed. "I believe I thought him quite the most splendidly hand-

284

some man in the whole regiment – aside from my father, that is!"

"H'm." It was an enigmatic sort of grunt, followed by silence.

Felicity waited expectantly. She stole a look at him; he was frowning. There were times when she wished he was less... complex! Surely he could say something – just a hint, even.

"Now, now, you two!" Sir Peregrine's voice brought them both back to a realization of where they were. "Max, you slow-top! What are you thinking about, prosing on at that poor girl when you should be whirling her around the floor. Look at young Tremaine there – only one arm and putting us all to shame!"

They all stood for a moment watching the quadrille in which Johnny was executing his entrechats with all the ease and skill demanded of one of the Duke of Wellington's officers, his gracefulness not one whit diminished by his lack of an arm. He looked up at that moment and seeing Felicity, grinned and made her an exaggerated salute.

"There, d'ye see, my boy?" said Sir Peregrine, preparing to depart for the games room. "Now, next time around, you show young Felicity here what you can do."

"Acquit me, uncle," said the Earl stiffly. "Felicity would find me a sad letdown, I believe. Dancing is not my forte. Your pardon." He strode away.

"Well now!" said Sir Peregrine, looking after him. "What do you make of that, young Felicity?"

Felicity knew exactly what to make of it. She had allowed a few empty compliments to go to her head. As common sense painfully reasserted itself she was astounded at her own naivete – to assume that one kiss, taken in a state of advanced inebriation, could ever constitute a basis for a deeper attachment! Why, it would be astonishing if he even remembered that incident, except perhaps with disgust. And the sooner she forgot it, the better!

She became aware of the little group

of rout chairs close by, where Mr. and Mrs. Lipscombe sat – and of the darting glance of triumph which the latter shot at her.

She blinked back the stinging tears and said lightly, "Why, it is as I thought, sir. Lord Stayne has better things to do than be dancing with me."

"Then he is a fool!" said his uncle.

No more so than I, she concluded miserably. It was manifestly obvious that being in love, like Jamie's measles, was a wretched experience from which only time would deliver her. She did not doubt her eventual recovery – people did not really die of broken hearts, after all. Only she had the oddest sensation that, unlike Jamie, she would never be quite whole again.

Chapter Thirteen

The small boy loomed up in the path of Felicity's gig so that she was obliged to rein in. He was one of the Manor Court children. She tried to call his name to mind; it was one of those unlikely, biblical names. He stood immobile – irresolute, heedless of the mist which lay like a pall over the whole village.

"Joshua?" The name came to her as she spoke. "Is there something you want?" In truth , she was wishing him far away. She had been late leaving school and wanted only to get home. Yet something about the boy impelled her to persist. "Don't be afraid, child."

"Please, miss. I heard you was looking for Lanny Price?"

Felicity's heart leaped. "You know where he is?"

The boy scuffed his feet. "Wouldn't

want to get 'im into trouble . . ."

"Of course Lanny won't get into trouble. I just want to find him."

"The drover's hut," muttered Joshua.

"On the common? Oh, but we searched there days ago!" The horse shied and she was obliged to calm him down before she could give the matter her full attention. "Are you sure, child?"

But the boy had gone, melting into the fine curtain of mist. Felicity sat on, uncertain what to do for the best. On a day that was more fitted to November than July, the prospect of venturing onto the bleak common was less than inviting; the more so when home meant the comfort of a blazing fire and a waiting tea tray. Lord Stayne wouldn't like it. He had been furious with her for visiting Manor Court alone; crass stupidity, he had called it. Not one word of concern about Dick Price's brutal murder – or for the missing Lanny. And she had been endowing him, in his absence, with such qualities of sympathy and understanding!

Well, if he didn't care, that was no reason for her to abdicate her responsibilities.

She knew that she could never settle while there was a chance of finding Lanny, so reluctantly she turned the gig and presently took the track near Ester's cottage, which led up onto the common.

It was unnaturally still, as though the mizzle was blanketing all sound. Patches of scrub and queer stunted trees reared up with eerie suddenness; a place for witches and hobgoblins! The fanciful turn of thought made her smile; she had been in many worse places, after all – and at least here no murdering, marauding bands of Gitanos would descend upon her! Any gypsies she had seen in England bore little resemblance to their black-avised Spanish brethren.

The drover's hut looked squat, deserted – and uninviting.

"Lanny?" she called softly, straining her ears for the least sound. Nothing.

Felicity climbed down and tethered the gelding to a tree stump. The mizzle was wetting. She drew her shawl around her shoulders. The door of the hut was stiff; a strong push and it swung inward with a spine-chilling groan.

"Lanny," she called again. The interior was dim, the only source of light a small, indescribably dirty window. The strip of gloomy daylight thrown inward by the open door illumined only a choice array of cobwebs showing little signs of having been disturbed in weeks, and a low, rickety-looking table thick with dust. There was little visible sign that Lanny had ever been here.

With a sigh she turned to leave. A slight sound made her pause; it was most probably a mouse or a rat, but it would be stupid to go without making sure.

Felicity pushed the door wider and stepped inside.

Her arms were instantly seized and before she could do more than turn to catch a glimpse of huge, dark shapes, her cries were stifled by a thick, foul-smelling sack which was thrown over her head and secured with terrifying thoroughness.

She was bundled at a run across the uneven floor, and spreadeagled face down across the spindly table which creaked ominously under the sudden shuddering impact.

Shock deprived her of immediate coherent thought, but with the return of her senses came a stark, primeval fear. Iron-hard fingers clamped her wrists to the rough board so that she was unable to move a muscle. The sack stifled sound and combined with her ignominious position made breathing difficult, yet she knew with frightening certainly that this was the least of her troubles.

After an eternity of inaction, a voice rasped close to her ear. It was the man, Rayner.

"You've had warnings enough, schoolteacher ... but you thought yourself too grand to heed them! That weren't clever ... not clever at all!"

A second voice joined in, deep, with a strong sing-song cadence. "Seems like we got to show you just how unhealthy dis place is fow de likes of you!"

Felicity knew what must happen next just as surely as she knew there was a third man in the room, though there was nothing but a flesh-creeping instinct to support her certainty.

There was a sudden draft as the wrap was plucked from her shoulders and quite distinctly, she heard a sharp intake of breath.

It seemed to act as a signal.

Her own breath was forced through clenched teeth in a series of small explosions as the lash bit with expert precision ... six ... seven ... eight times. She wondered dully how long she could bite back the scream that rose in her throat with each stinging, humiliating stroke ... she remembered the soldiers she had seen flogged – and tried to recall how long it had taken them to reach that state of gibbering insensibility which had so appalled her ...

And then it was over. Silence enveloped her; a thick, woolly silence where pain, wild and throbbing, was the only reality.

A voice penetrated the woolliness, distorted but unmistakably Hardman's.

"That was just a small lesson, schoolmarm! Learn it well! You won't be offered any second chances. Close your school, pack your belongings – and go."

Felicity lay inert, listening to them leave. It took a monumental effort to drag herself upright, to steady herself against the table before lifting numbed fingers to untie the sack. The rank air in the hut was like heady wine; she drank it in greedily while her eyes adjusted to the light – and the sounds of drumming hoofbeats died away. She stooped stiffly to pick up her shawl and walked to the door, lifting her face with relief to the blessed, refreshing rain.

She managed to reach the privacy of her room without meeting anyone, locked the door, and sat on the bed – and found that she was shaking. She leaned her arms along the brass rail at the foot of the bed, put down her head – and wept.

Later, her tears spent, she was calm again. A preliminary and somewhat painful exploration of her condition decided her that she would need help. The back of her dress was ripped in several places and would need to be eased away.

Felicity found a maid and sent her in search of Rose Hibberd. When Rose came, Felicity locked the door behind her. "I need your help, Rose. But I want your promise that what passes in this room will go no further."

Rose looked bewildered . . . and hesitated.

"It is nothing dishonest, that much I swear to you. But it touches no one other than myself, and I would keep it that way. Do I have your word, Rose?"

Rose didn't like Miss Vale's white face, the desperate entreaty in her eyes. She was in trouble – that was for sure!

"Yes, miss," she said quietly. "If that's the way you want it."

When she saw Felicity's back, however, she blenched. "Oh, God love you, miss!" she gasped. "Whoever would do such a thing to you?"

"That isn't important now, Rose. If you could just help me off with my dress?"

Even with care, this proved to be an uncomfortable experience for both young women; by the time they were done, Felicity was whiter than ever; her jaw bunched into rigidity.

"How bad is it, Rose?"

Rose's voice was shaky. "Well, miss – the skin's only broken in a couple of places, but the rest is swollen something awful. You ought to see the doctor, really you ought!"

"No!" Felicity walked across to the chest of drawers and withdrew a small leather case which traveled everywhere with her. "I have a liniment . . . excellent stuff . . . better than anything Dr. Belvedere could prescribe. If you would be so kind as to apply it for me? And again in the morning?"

"Yes, of course I will, miss."

As she was leaving, Rose hesitated, her nice, homely face very earnest. "But you will tell his lordship, miss?"

"No!" Again Felicity was very positive.

"Well, if you ask me," Rose persisted, "whoever did that – and I've got my suspicions – they need calling to account. Oh, I'll hold my peace, miss – I've given my word and I'll not go back on it, but I don't have to approve!"

Lord Stayne was out of temper. He had been to see Sir Geoffrey Blunt to discover at first hand what had been going on in his absence. It had been an unsatisfactory visit. Sir Geoffrey was not a man he cared for overmuch, either personally or as a magistrate. On the few occasions they had shared the bench, he had found him to be boorish, intractable, and full of prejudice.

His attitude toward Price's death had been depressingly predictable. The stand he was taking over the attempted barn-burnings was more worrying. He was friendly with Hardman, which had not endeared him to the locals; but more damaging was his official opinion, that it was the work of radical dissidents, enemies of His Majesty's established Government, and part of a much wider plot to overthrow the Government. As such, it would not be tolerated. The culprits would be rooted out and a lasting example made of them!

Since the Earl could find no grounds for believing they were dealing with anything more dangerous than a few local people with a grievance, he was understandably furious. Not only were such assumptions unjust, they had wilfully damaged the goodwill which he had always sought to maintain in the district. Now, for the first time, he encountered sullen looks, and that boded ill for the future, for once a sense of injustice was allowed to fester, men ceased to discriminate and all authority could be threatened.

Angry preoccupation made him careless, so that he negotiated the entrance to

Cheynings at a pace which almost resulted in a coat of paint being shaved from the curricle's bright yellow wheels and caused Percy to draw in a soundless whistle.

Whew! That was close! Not the guv'nor's usual style when trying out a brand-new team!

It was usually a pleasure to sit up behind him ... but not today. 'Course, he could always tell by the set of his lordship's head and the way his ears went pink.! In a proper miff 'e was today and no mistake! He'd not been best pleased when they'd left Sir Geoffrey's house, and a visit to Manor Court hadn't improved matters. Downright surly that Rayner'd been ... in fact, Percy was willing to swear as he'd been scared silly on seeing the guv'nor ... He'd been pretty quick to insist that the Captain wasn't home. Just as well, too, p'raps ...

Stayne gave the horses their heads down the carriageway, but took no more than a perfunctory interest in the excellence of their performance. He was still badly rattled by that appalling error of judgment. How Felicity would have roasted him! Or would she? He was no longer sure and the thought gave him pain. Since the morning following the ball, when they had clashed with more than usual violence, she had studiously avoided him. He was astonished to discover just how much her behavior affected him, the more so as he had come upon her on more than one occasion riding with Tremaine in the early morning, their ready laughter floating on the air.

And then there was her indisposition; Felicity was not the type to suffer "slight indispositions." Much more of such behavior and he would tax her with it – he had done so before, had he not? But that had been a long time ago . . . many things had changed . . .

He dragged his attention back to the horses. For once the weather was kind – a rare enough occurrence in this torrentially rainy summer. The sun slanted in mocking brilliance through the trees, dappling the road ahead with ever-changing patterns, highlighting their rippling bodies.

Along the shaded verge, as though contemptuous of the sun's flirtatious overtures, trudged a small figure, weary, yet with an air of determination.

The Earl reined in just ahead of him – and waited.

"Well, Lanny?" he demanded coldly as the lad came abreast and trailed to a halt.

Lanny stared back. His smock was crumpled and filthy, his red hair stood up in defiant spikes, and the translucent white skin with its splattering of freckles, so typical of his coloring, was stretched paper-thin across the bones of his face, making his eyes very blue – and apprehensive.

He swallowed and looked down at his feet. " . . . want to see Miss Vale," he muttered.

"Do you, indeed? Well, I want to see you!"

The boy's head jerked up convulsively. "I ain't done nothin' to you. You can't . . ."

"Oh yes I can, lad. You've caused a lot of people a lot of trouble. Now I want some answers. No – don't try to run away again. There's been enough of that. Why have you been hiding all this time?"

"Reasons."

"You talk civil to 'is lordship," Percy said sharply.

Stayne frowned and gestured him to silence. His own voice softened a little. "Was it because of your father?" he continued, and saw the boy flinch. "Yes, I know about your father. Were you with him that night?"

Lanny was still poised like a taut spring. "I'll do a deal with you," he offered, while desperation grew in his eyes.

The Earl's lips twitched. "You aren't exactly in a strong bargaining position, lad."

"Oh, but this is something you'll want to know, something only I can tell you," Lanny wheedled. "It's why I wanted to see Miss Vale... only p'raps you'd be better."

His ingenuous attempt at negotiation diverted Stayne. "Right," he said. "Come on, then."

Lanny's eyes opened wide as saucers. "You mean... up there? Ride with you?"

"Well, I've certainly no intention of letting you out of my sight again." The Earl's voice was dry.

To Percy's disgust, Lord Stayne reached down a hand and Lanny grasped it with eager, clawlike fingers and was hoisted up.

Chapter Fourteen

Rose was on her way upstairs when the Earl waylaid her.

"Good evening, Rose. How is Miss Vale this evening? Still indisposed?"

His manner was bland, yet she found herself blushing under that uncomfortably penetrating eye.

"No ... not exactly, my lord ... that is, she's better than she was ..." Her voice trailed away.

"Ah! Then be good enough to ask her if she will spare me a few minutes of her time before she retires. I shall be in the crimson salon."

Felicity received the summons with something less than enthusiasm. The liniment had eased the worst of her soreness, but a near-sleepless night and a day of discomfort had left her physically drained and bruised in spirit.

She toyed with the idea of sending back a message declaring herself unfit, but suspected that Stayne was more than likely to call her bluff.

The crimson salon was bathed in soft pink light. Beyond the windows the setting sun had suffused the sky with a blushing glory, setting everything aflame. The light should have been kind to Felicity; it did indeed turn her cream wrapper to a more delicate hue and tinged her pallid cheeks with color, but it also emphasized the enormous smudges which made her eyes seem luminous by comparison.

"I am sorry to know you have been unwell," Stayne said in an odd voice, after subjecting her to an uncompromising scrutiny. "I trust you are feeling more . . . restored?"

"Thank you, yes."

"You don't look it," he said with brutal frankness. "Pray sit down."

He indicated one of the armchairs near the fire, but she declined, finding it easier to perch upon one of the occasional chairs set about the room, careful to choose one which did not face the light. She hoped he would not keep her long.

"My dear girl," the Earl remarked, "are you perfectly comfortable there? You look ill-at-ease. Is there something you wish to tell me, perhaps?"

Drat the man! He was too omniscient by far! With a supreme effort she refrained from wincing as she eased herself into what she hoped would appear a more relaxed position.

"No, my lord," she said. "I cannot imagine why you should think it."

The note of defiance was not lost on him; he continued to observe her as he poured himself a glass of brandy – and another, smaller one which he handed to her.

"Drink it!" he commanded. "It will do you good. I would not have put you to the trouble of coming down, but I wanted your opinion upon a story that I heard today."

Felicity stirred fretfully, grimacing

over the brandy. "Really, sir – I don't . . ."

"Patience, Miss Vale. This story should interest you, I think. It concerns a young woman very like yourself – a schoolteacher, foolish enough to make enemies and vain enough to imagine herself capable of dealing with those enemies!"

Felicity flushed and bit her lip. He only addressed her as Miss Vale in that cutting way when he wished to be offensive, but in her present state of mental inertia she declined to pursue the cause.

"The similarity does not end there," he continued. "This schoolteacher also had a problem pupil – a boy addicted to poaching. After numerous warnings there was one final, rather ugly incident and the boy took fright and disappeared."

A cold feeling was settling in the pit of Felicity's stomach; a hurried sip of brandy scorched its way down and brought stinging tears to her eyes, but did little to warm her. Somehow, he knew!

"The schoolteacher must have been given a message that the child had taken refuge in an isolated, disused hut. She went, alone – a most foolhardy act, for there her enemies awaited her."

He went on to describe what had followed in such vivid detail that she began to tremble, remembering. She gripped the glass hard and by the time he had finished, her head was bent, the heavy curtain of her hair veiling her face.

Out of the silence, the Earl's voice came harshly. "Well, Felicity Vale? You say nothing. I have shocked you, perhaps? Come – I am eager for your opinion – a horrifying tale, it is not?"

"Horrifying," she agreed, with only the slightest of tremors. "Of course, I do not know your source, my lord, but I would venture to suggest that, like many good dramatic stories, it has gained in the telling."

"Then you would be wrong," he said curtly. "Indeed, I have considerably abridged the original evocative prose! My informant was intimately concerned, you see – and was understandably distressed."

"Lanny!" Felicity exclaimed, looking up involuntarily.

"Precisely. It preyed on his mind that he had watched the whole from the window without lifting a finger to help."

"Oh, poor Lanny! There was nothing he could have done."

"Why, so I told him when his guilt finally drove him to unburden himself. As it happens, he was seeking you – but found me!"

"Is he all right? Can I see him? Will he get into trouble?"

"All in good time."

The sun had gone down, taking with it all warmth, all kindness. Stayne lit the candles and turned to stare down at her.

"Why did you not tell me?"

"Because . . ." She would not meet his eyes. "Oh, well . . . because it was a harrowing and . . . yes, a humiliating experience; hardly one I would care to broadcast. But that is all – you are making too much of the incident."

"I see." Felicity wished he wouldn't tower over her. "So you were not hurt overmuch?"

"Only in my pride," she insisted stubbornly.

He stooped and before she knew what he was about had gripped her shoulders and was forcing her gently, but quite inescapably, against the intricate scrollwork of the chairback. She stiffened as the eddies of pain quivered across her bruised flesh. The pressure eased at once, yet he still held her effectively a prisoner, her very closeness – the accusing whiteness of her face – seeming to fan his anger.

"Liar!" he said softly. "How bad is it, really?"

"Quite tolerable," she gasped. "When it is not violently abused."

"Oh, I have no doubt you think me cruel, but Hardman used you far more brutally, did he not? And will do so again to gain his objective."

"But why? The school does him no harm! There is no reason . . ."

"Reason? A man like Hardman does not reason! If you have learned nothing else from this affair, you should have learned that much. It no longer matters why he ever wanted the school closed. Now – you are the thorn in his flesh. He desires nothing less than your total submission, and he will stick at nothing to achieve the end!"

"Then he will not succeed!"

The Earl straightened up and moved away with an air of finality. "Fortunately, Miss Vale, the decision is not yours to make."

Felicity followed him and caught at his sleeve. "No. You cannot mean to give in? What about the village? What about the children?"

"They will survive." His jaw was rigidly uncompromising.

"Of course they will survive! But it isn't like passing out sweetmeats, you know . . . it may have been no more than a whim to you, but that school is now the center of their life. They are going to feel bitterly disappointed and let down . . ."

"Will you have done!" He swung around in a fury, shaking her off. "You talk about giving in, as though it were a game! Well, if it is, it is a damnable one. In God's name, what do you expect me to do? Wait until your body turns up in the river as Lanny's father did? For, make no mistake, that will be the end of it!"

"Oh, stuff! You are being absurdly melodramatic!" she flung at him.

"And you, Felicity Vale, are a willful, stubborn young woman! Quite as bad as Hardman in your way. How much is your passion a genuine care for the village and how much an obstinate determination not to be bested?"

"Oh!" She put up a hand as though he had struck her, and then with a stifled sob she ran from the room. Behind her she heard him call, "Felicity – wait!" but she didn't stop running until she reached her room.

The angry, fruitless tears were soon

spent, and though she passed another uncomfortable night, by morning she was full of resolution. The sun slanted in early, adding a fillip to that resolution. She came down to find that Lord Stayne had already breakfasted and gone.

She ran Lord Stayne to earth at last in the gun room deep in a discussion with Perkins. On seeing her he dismissed the keeper.

The Earl's look was not encouraging, so she came straight to the point.

"I thought you should know, my lord, I intend to leave here at the end of the week."

The Earl looked disconcerted. "That will not be necessary."

"I cannot agree, sir."

His voice was harsh. "Are you then so eager to shake the dust of Cheynings from your feet?"

"No!" Felicity was stung. "But you have dispensed with my services as a schoolteacher, and Jamie now has his tutor. There is no longer any place for me here."

He looked into her resolute face and found the prospect of life at Cheynings without her infinitely dreary. "Nonsense," he said abruptly. "Whatever happens, your place here is assured, as well you know."

"Thank you, my lord," she returned with spirit. "But I will not be your pensioner, as well you know."

"Still that deuced independence?" His glance softened curiously. "I wish you would not be so absurd."

"I am sorry if I seem so."

"Then stay," he urged. "Reconsider. You are being too hasty."

For a moment it almost seemed that he would say more, but Felicity was already shaking her head. "It is better that I go. There are reasons . . . and Johnny will be leaving at the weekend. I can travel with him."

"I see," he said curtly.

Felicity hesitated and then held out her hand in an impulsive gesture. Her bones melted instantly at his touch. She said a trifle unsteadily, "But I thank you

314

for the offer . . . and for . . . for showing such tolerance of my odd ways."

"I have not been in the least tolerant!" He regarded the hand, long-fingered and capable, as it lay in his own. "I was not tolerant last night. Indeed, I behaved in a way which . . . but you will allow my patience to have been tried beyond endurance?"

"The circumstances were exceptional," Felicity agreed faintly and tried, unsuccessfully, to withdraw her hand. "I must go. I have to see Ester . . . to explain . . ."

His eyes lifted to rake her face. "No use, I suppose, to insist that you are scarcely fit?"

"I am well enough, sir!"

"Will you at least allow that I have usually had your best interests at heart?"

"Yes, my lord."

"Then you don't have to go," he said. "No, let me finish. You see I too have been doing some thinking."

Felicity's heart was beginning to beat in her throat.

"The school is to close for the whole of August, is it not?" She nodded, mystified. "We are already well through July; so, if you were to finish tomorrow instead of next week, it would cause little comment."

Her momentary foolishness drained away. If only he would release her, she thought illogically, there would be no temptation to indulge her fancies.

"While I was away," he continued, "I made a few discreet inquiries about our friend Hardman. He is a clever man, but not clever enough. He had a partner who died, and that death was not the accident it seemed. I have lodged my findings with Bow Street and I suspect that the district will be rid of the Captain long before September."

"Oh, but that is marvelous! I knew you would rout him eventually."

The Earl was quizzical. "Your faith in me is touching, if premature. Our villain is not yet apprehended, and I don't want him frightened off. I am to see him later today; what I mean to say to him concerning recent events should occupy his attention more than adequately until the Runners arrive. But you see what this means?" His hand tightened. "The school's future is secure – and you need not leave."

Felicity did not answer. She did not know how to answer. Every instinct told her she must go. He could make nothing of her expression.

"At all events, promise me that you will not venture out unaccompanied over the next few days?" he urged. "I don't trust Hardman."

"Oh, but . . ."

"No buts, Felicity. Your promise, if you please."

Whether he knew it or not, his hand was now crushing hers. "Very well," she agreed, remembering that cold threatening voice. "Johnny will be happy to stand duty."

"Someone taking my name in vain?" Johnny stood in the doorway. Stayne dropped Felicity's hand abruptly.

Johnny strolled into the room, eyeing

the racks of guns appreciatively.

He grinned at Felicity. "Would it be infernally inquisitive in me to wish to know what it is I should be happy to do?"

"Act as my escort," Felicity replied promptly.

"Charmed, my dear girl, but since when have you needed an escort?"

"It seems I need one now."

"The village is in a state of unrest," put in the Earl, uncommunicatively. "One man, in particular, has a grudge against Felicity . . ."

"That fellow Hardman? The one Sir Peregrine talked of?" Johnny's eyebrows lifted. "You think he might make trouble?"

Felicity looked embarrassed.

"He has already tried," said Stayne grimly. "I am not prepared to offer him any further opportunity."

Johnny made an elaborate leg to Felicity. "Then behold me at your service, ma'am. I am yours to command."

"Idiot!" she laughed.

318

Stayne viewed their play-acting with tightened lips. "This is no light-hearted romp," he snapped. "You will do better to let me put one of the grooms at your disposal, Felicity. The one I have in mind is a big, strong lad – well able to take care of himself – and you."

Johnny's face was blank, but just for an instant Felicity, who knew him so well, had seen his eyes flare with raw anguish at his implied inadequacy. It filled her with helpless anger and pity and this, together with a fierce pride in the regiment, drew her close to him, to say coldly: "Thank you, my lord, but I would back Johnny, one arm or no, against any two of your grooms!"

They stood ranged against him – the fair, handsome soldier with more bottom than one would suspect on first acquaintance, and an invincible auburn-haired girl with so-expressive eyes, who could match her soldier for height and more than match him in courage – two people, totally dissimilar at a glance, yet two of a kind, bound together by something more than affection – a whole life-time of shared experiences; it made an impregnable bond.

Johnny turned to Felicity, his smile twisted. "Thank you, m'dear, for the vote of confidence, but Stayne is in the right of it, you know."

He moved away deliberately to investigate the gun cases around the wall. "I envy you some of these, my lord," he said, his elegant finger touching a slim fowling piece with loving sensitivity.

Felicity's eyes met the Earl's. There was a mute appeal in their blazing depths which he could not ignore.

"This one is new." He tossed the gun and Johnny turned and caught it deftly, testing its balance expertly, exclaiming over the beautifully worked stock.

"It's one of Manton's, of course."

"Yes. I had it specially made. It incorporates several interesting refinements." The Earl paused. "You must come and see it in action sometime – when your escort duties permit."

Johnny's head lifted. The two men looked steadily at one another. Then Johnny nodded – and grinned. "Thanks," he said laconically.

Felicity approached her return to school with misgivings.

Ester was pleased to see her, but said bluntly, "You look as if you shouldn't be here! I could have managed, you know."

"My dear Ester," said Felicity dryly, "I do know it! You can run this place every bit as well as I – better probably. But there were reasons why I needed to come."

Ester looked at her sharply. "It's true, then. The rumor about the school closing?"

"No! That is ... no." Her very indecisiveness must have seemed halfway to an admission. She hastened to correct her error, yet quite stupidly shrank from telling Ester the whole – for the moment it was all too painfully fresh in her mind. Of her determination to leave, she said nothing.

Instead she stuck to the essentials . . . the intended early closure of the school and the Earl's conviction that he had the means to rid the district of Captain Hardman for good. This brought an exclamation, but Felicity hurried on, before awkward questions could be asked, with the news that Lanny had turned up unhurt – and that she now had great hopes that the Earl would actively help the boy. At any rate, he was to stay at the Home Farm for the time being, out of harm's way, getting a few good meals inside him.

By midafternoon Felicity's back was aching abominably.

By the time Johnny came for her, she was ready to fall upon his neck. He looked her over with the eye of a seasoned campaigner.

"Exhausted," was the laconic verdict. "In you get, m'dear . . . if I don't get you home soon, I shall be drummed out for dereliction of duty!"

Felicity smiled diffidently, "Johnny – I beg you will not refine too much upon what Lord Stayne said. He can be out-spoken."

Johnny gave her a withering look – and then looked closer and whistled softly. "So that's the way of it!" he murmured.

She flushed a painful scarlet, but was saved a reply by a sudden commotion behind them. They turned to see smoke; a great shout of "Fire!" echoed down the green.

"It's the schoolhouse!" cried Felicity. "We must go back!"

Johnny wheeled the gig, cursing his missing arm, and urged the reluctant gelding back toward the fire.

Women were already running for pails or anything else which would hold water. Some were already at the pump.

The school's thatched roof was well alight and flames were licking up the windows at the near end. It was here that most of the water was being indiscriminately flung.

"They'll never contain it that way!" Johnny tied the horse securely and strode off to bring order to the proceedings. "Thank God for the wet summer – at least it lessens the risk of the fire spreading!"

Felicity ran on, her tiredness forgotten, fear for the children superceding all else. She pushed her way through the growing crush of people and found Ester in the midst of a babble of youngsters.

"Are they all out? she shouted, grasping her arm.

Ester turned a haunted face. "Yes . . . yes! But I can't find my two! Someone must have them!"

She shook off Felicity's arm and plunged into the crowd. Felicity's heart turned over and she too began asking questions of people too preoccupied to care.

A small girl tugged diffidently at her arm, "Please, miss – I seen Willie Graham."

"Where?" The question was unintentionally sharp and tears of fright made dirty streaks down the child's face. Felicity cursed her own impatience and stooped to encourage her. "Please, Lily – where did you see him?"

"He . . . he was going into the school, miss." Lily sniffed and licked her lips. "He had the little 'un with him."

Oh, dear God! "When was this?" She forced calmness into her voice, when she longed to scream.

Another sniff. "Dunno, miss. Not long."

Felicity swung away in despair, seeking Ester throughout the anthill of figures scurrying about in the drifting pall of smoke. Men were coming in all the time from the outlying parts of the estate and Johnny was busy organizing them into an efficient fire-fighting team with the same calm cheerfulness he brought to commanding a troop of cavalry. He saw her and lifted a hand in salute; his teeth gleamed white against a dirt-streaked face.

Her agony of indecision lasted seconds and seemed like hours. It would be useless to tell Johnny – besides, Willie would come for no one save Ester or herself.

She ran across to the chain of women passing pails from hand to hand and implored them to soak her in water. The women gaped, uncomprehending, and Felicity seized a pail impatiently. The initial impact of the water made her gasp, but was as nothing compared to the wall of heat which met her inside the building.

Even with her shawl pulled across the lower half of her face, the acrid smoke snatched at her throat; it stabbed her eyes with red-hot needles until they streamed. At first she could see nothing. Hoarsely she called the children . . . and then she saw them at the far end of the room where her desk stood. The fire had not yet spread that far, except for the roof, which was well ablaze. Felicity picked her way toward them, side-stepping to avoid the occasional fireball which fell hissing to the floor.

They were a sorry-looking pair, blackened by smuts. Little Jenny sat whimpering on the floor, coughing and rubbing at red eyes, her bright curls unrecognizable, while her brother stood, seemingly impervious to discomfort, watching the flames and clutching his precious ball, which must have been left behind in the rush to leave.

"Red ball," he said, when Felicity reached them, and she knew that his poor mind was incapable of recognizing danger. "Red," he said again, pointing to the flames.

Felicity lifted the baby, tucking her safely beneath the shawl. She took Willie's hand. "Come along, now," she said gently. "We must go."

Near the door where the smoke was thickest, her dress snagged on something. She tugged and pulled, but with both hands occupied, she was unable to free herself. They were all beginning to choke now; every second was precious. She set Jenny down and put her hand into Willie's.

"You must take your sister outside, Willie – quickly, now! I will follow you in a moment." Felicity willed him to understand and obey, and for once he did. She pushed them toward the door and turned with streaming eyes to free her dress. It was firmly caught on a jagged piece of wood between two broken desks. She pulled it loose and in rising, found a blessedly familiar figure filling the doorway.

"Max!" In her relief she called his name.

His face was distorted by the smoke; he was shouting something, his hand gesturing urgently.

She looked up, too late to avoid the blazing beam which came crashing toward her.

Chapter Fifteen

She awoke to pain. Every inch of her body throbbed with it; her eyelids were weighted with lead; her mind fuzzy and tumbled in confusion.

Voices came and went, some vaguely familiar . . .

"Is she badly hurt? . . . My God, I thought she was dead when you brought her out! . . . That's a nasty crack on the head . . . Oh, but her beautiful hair . . ."

Hands were moving over her, feather-light hands – infinitely gentle, yet every touch sent fresh waves of agony pulsating through her . . . a voice she knew now . . . a voice she wanted to hear more than any other . . . sounding harsher than she had ever heard it . . .

"No bones broken, but that cursed beam's put her shoulder out! Where the hell is Belvedere?"

She wanted to tell him not to fuss, but the words kept getting lost in an evil-smelling fog ... it set her throat on fire ...

Fire! Of course!

"The children?" It came out as a feeble croak, but the effect on her audience was quite astonishing. Encouraged, she made a supreme effort and forced her aching eyes open.

She was lying out in the open, looking up at the sky through a drifting, sluggish haze. Johnny was there ... and Ester ... others, too ... their faces grimy, like sweeps.

One face swam close – so close that she very much wanted to smooth her fingers along that livid scar. His eyes were intensely black, as though he were angry with her.

"Sorry." The croak was a bit better that time, but he looked fiercer than ever.

"Don't try to talk! The children are safe – and the fire is out."

Her eyelids were growing too heavy to

stay open. She drifted away and the voices went on murmuring above her . . . until Stayne's voice suddenly snapped her back to full consciousness.

"Devil take the man! He can't be away now!"

"Couldn't you do it?" Johnny's voice now, hesitant. "I've put many a shoulder back in my time, before . . ."

"So have I, Major – on the hunting field! But this is different. I can't do it!"

That could not be Max? She had never heard such a rasping note of despair from him. It seemed important to reassure him.

"Yes, you can," she whispered, attempting levity. "I would as lief . . . not . . . lie here all night!"

"Felicity!" His eyes were agonized, but she knew his decision was already made and she tried to smile encouragement.

They insisted on giving her brandy, which set her throat on fire again.

"Hold on to my hand, old thing," Johnny said in a distinctly odd voice.

She had thought she knew all about pain, but this was a new dimension altogether! When it was over, they poured more brandy down her throat and bound her arm tight to her side. And then she was jolted home in the gig, held close by Stayne, with her face turned in to his neck. At one point she must have been delirious, for she groaned and thought he murmured "Hush, my dear love!" and brushed her cheek with his lips.

Then events became more confused than ever. There was Jamie's scared face and Uncle Perry's strangely puckered one . . . and Amaryllis crying, "Oh, Max – her hair!" . . . the second time someone had said that. . . . There was talk of scissors, and Max saying roughly, "Do it now – before she is put to bed." And the vile scissors began snipping away inexorably.

She cried then, for the first time – sobbing bitterly into his coat, for they were cutting off her lovely hair.

"Oh . . . oh, I'm sorry," she hiccuped.

"You hate tears, I know! It m-must be all that brandy."

Stayne swore. "Your hair will grow again," he insisted fiercely.

After that, she remembered very little until she awoke to find the late afternoon sun flooding in through gently floating muslin curtains to highlight cheerful hangings sprigged with primroses. Amaryllis sat beside the bed, laboriously stitching a lace border to a handkerchief. She threw it aside as Felicity stirred.

"Well, thank goodness!" she exclaimed. "I had begun to think you would never wake up!"

"This isn't my room." Felicity frowned, turning her head on the pillow, and finding it a surprisingly uncomfortable exercise.

"No. We have moved you into the yellow bedchamber. I couldn't be climbing all those stairs every five minutes!"

A faint smile flickered. "How . . . long have I been here?"

"Three days. Dr. Belvedere thought

your total collapse a delayed reaction – in fact, your powers of endurance have astonished him, and in view of everything I'm bound to..." Here Amaryllis stopped. Embarrassment flickered across the perfect features. "Max told us... about Captain Hardman... well, he had to, for we saw your poor back! Oh, Felicity, however did you survive such a dreadful experience? Without a word to any of us! And then the fire..."

Felicity tried to remember, to raise some degree of feeling, but it all seemed a long time ago.

"Did the fire do much damage?"

"Lud! The place is a blackened ruin... the roof gone completely. You were lucky not to have been killed!"

The anger was gone, but a great sadness enveloped Felicity. How much had it been her fault? Perhaps, if she had been less stubborn...? "So Captain Hardman won, after all – in the end," she said aloud.

"But no! He has gone. You missed quite a drama, I can tell you! Max was riding to Manor Court, you know, when he saw the smoke coming from the village. He rushed over and arrived only just in time to drag you out alive!" Amaryllis was almost incoherent with the recollection. "When he had brought you safely home, he stormed out of the house! I have never seen Max so enraged! Johnny went after him. I truly believe he feared Max meant to kill Hardman!"

"Oh, no!" A terrible panic filled her.

"He was too late!" Amaryllis said triumphantly. "Someone had seen the men who started the fire running away – and recognized them as Hardman's men. So practically the whole village marched on Manor Court and set fire to it in retaliation."

"Oh, but they should not . . . it was a wicked thing to do! The consequences . . ."

"Oh, pooh!" said Amaryllis. "One cannot prosecute a whole village! And it was no more than he deserved."

Felicity tried to sit up and groaned at

finding even this simple feat beyond her. "Was anyone killed?"

"Only a man called Rayner. The rest turned tail and ran. Mind you, Johnny reckoned that Hardman would have been massacred if he and Max had not arrived when they did. They found him cowering in an outhouse with his son . . . and the crowd outside baying for his blood!" She shuddered delicately.

Tears of weakness welled up in Felicity's eyes. Amaryllis rushed to pour some cordial and persuaded her cousin to drink a little.

"I shall be shot for upsetting you! Pray, don't trouble your head any further. That horrid man is certainly not worth your tears! Besides, Max insisted that he be given a carriage and allowed to leave. Johnny did not hear all that was said between them – something about a murder inquiry and Bow Street Runners. Whatever it was, Hardman left – a quivering jelly of a man – and will never return."

So it was all over.

As Felicity slowly regained her strength, she was not short of company. Ester came often, her quiet gratitude saying so much more than mere words, but she never brought the children, and behind her eyes there still lingered the haunting sense of guilt that it was her son who had so nearly caused Felicity's death.

Uncle Perry had been shattered by all that had happened. He had been on the point of leaving for London, but delayed his departure until he had reassured himself that she was well on the mend. When he finally came to say goodbye, Felicity thought he looked older.

"You take care, now," he admonished her.

"I will." She stroked his coat. "You are looking very splendid this afternoon."

"Looks well, don't it?" he enthused, momentarily diverted. Then he bent to peck her cheek. "Don't know what Max is thinking about?" he muttered. "Didn't even put a bullet in the fellow – would have done in my day!"

"Well, I am very glad he didn't," she said weakly. "I would not have that on my conscience."

Johnny spent a lot of time with her – so, too, did Jamie. Their uninhibited cheerfulness did much to bolster her flagging spirits. But the person she most wanted, came only once to ask formally after her health and departed from that formality for but a moment to observe brusquely that she looked like Jamie with her shortcropped curls.

Felicity kept to her room long after she might have returned to the family fold. There was a small balcony where she could sit when the weather permitted – and very occasionally she would take a walk.

Her lethargy persisted until the day Jamie came bounding onto her bed with the slightly incoherent announcement that Mamma was to marry Major Tremaine. "Isn't that the most tremendous news? I am to live with them in London. I expect I shall enjoy that no end! Mr.

338

Burnett is to come, too, but later on, Uncle Max says I may go away to school as he and my father did! And I may come here whenever I please. What do you think of that, Cousin F'licity?"

Amaryllis and Johnny followed close on his heels. "I gather the little wretch has stolen our thunder." Johnny looked like the cat who'd been at the cream pot – and Amaryllis was so obviously happy that any reservations Felicity might have had vanished on the instant.

"Oh, my dears, I am so happy for you!" She held out her hands to them. "I couldn't be more pleased!"

"Johnny is selling out and we shall live near Town. Just fancy – Max has retained the little house in Chelsea all this time. He is to make us a present of it – besides a most handsome settlement for Jamie's future. He feels that Johnny is just the father Jamie needs, and is quite agreeable to his coming with us, so we shall be a complete family."

Felicity knew a pang of jealousy, instantly stifled.

On the following evening there was a celebration dinner, which she made an effort to attend.

Amid the buzz of conversation following upon the Earl's toast to the happy couple, she overheard Mrs. Lipscombe confiding to a neighbor that she had every expectation of her daughter's being the next in line to be congratulated. "For I do not scruple to tell you, ma'am," she gushed, "that I believe it to have been no more than a proper sense of responsibility toward his sister-in-law which has until now held back the Earl's declaration!"

Felicity slipped away unnoticed. Beyond the doorway she encountered Lord Stayne, and her pallor, which all evening had vied with the ivory foulard of her dress, grew the more remarkable so that her eyes appeared huge and shadowed.

"Felicity?" He grasped her arm and his touch burned her skin. "You are unwell. Let me assist you to your room. This has all been too much for you."

Indeed it had. "No, sir. I thank you," she forced a bright smile to her lips. "I have enjoyed myself immensely, but I am now a little tired."

He looked her over comprehensively and his jaw tightened. "Liar!" he said with soft vehemence. "I know what ails you. Would to God there was something I could do to make it right for you!"

Felicity didn't try to make sense of his words; she snatched her arm away and ran.

Two days later a letter came from Mollie Patterson; it was like an answer to prayer. Felicity replied at once and made her plans.

When Amaryllis was told, however, she was appalled – and then tearful. "But you cannot leave now – today – just like that! You are not fit! Oh, what am I to do? Johnny has gone shooting with Max ... You cannot leave me to face them with the news!"

"I have left a note for Lord Stayne."

"But you mean to come back?"

Felicity looked around the room which was home, and had once seemed so grand. How long ago it was – that first dreadful day when she had felt herself an alien in a hostile place! So much had changed since then – she had changed . . .

"I don't think I will," she said abruptly. "I can hardly stay here with you and Jamie gone."

"Fudge! You have done so before."

Felicity shook her head. "That was different."

"Then live with Ester . . . she would have you, if you cannot stomach Max – you know she would!" Amaryllis was too upset to see the effect her words had. "Besides, there is your school."

"Ester can run the school very well without me now." The words were falsely bright. "No – I mean to stay with Mrs. Patterson for a while and then make a new start elsewhere."

Amaryllis was genuinely crying now. "But I wanted you at my wedding . . . and if you go, we shall lose you . . . I know we shall! Oh, I don't see why you must run off in this hole-and-corner fashion!"

Felicity flung her arms around her cousin and swallowed back her own tears. "It is the best way for me, my dear. Perhaps I have been a traveler too long to settle anywhere. But I promise to write, and I will come and stay with you in Chelsea."

The gentlemen returned a little earlier than expected. Cavanah gave Lord Stayne the note from Miss Vale and informed him that Mrs. Delamere wished to see them in the drawing room. Max looked vaguely puzzled, but did not immediately open the letter.

In the drawing room they found Amaryllis almost prostrate. Johnny went to her side. Her mouth trembled visibly as she broke the news.

"Gone," said the Earl blankly. "She can't have gone. She is not fit to travel."

"Why, so I told her, but she would have none of it," wailed Amaryllis. "You know how determined Felicity can be!"

"I do indeed!" He tore open the letter. The others watched his face as he read. "When did she go?"

"Benson has driven her into Stapleforth to catch the four o'clock stage."

There was a purposeful gleam in Stayne's eye as he glanced at the clock and strode to the door. "Then I must go if I am to be in time."

It was market day and Stapleforth was at its most chaotic. The Earl was obliged to maneuver his curricle through the crowded thoroughfare without the benefit of his young tiger's strident tongue to facilitate his progress.

His decision to travel without Percy had been the cause of much interested speculation in his stable yard as the dust settled in the wake of his departure . . . for had Benson not driven off with Miss Vale only a half hour previous, and her looking properly moped!

The clock on the Norman tower of the church wanted ten minutes to four as he swept under the archway into the teeming yard of the Swan Inn. Here all was

344

noise and bustle, for the stage had not long preceded him. Ostlers scurried back and forth; the sweating horses were being led away and a fresh team stood ready to be put to.

Passengers leaving the coach were fussily arranging the safe disposal of their baggage and calling for porters, but the Earl's glance strayed beyond them to scan the small group waiting patiently to board.

She was obliging enough to be standing a little apart from the rest, her shoulders drooping disconsolately, the inevitable guitar and shabby portmanteau at her feet.

He swung around to rein in beside her and sprang down, summoning a lad to hold the horses.

Felicity's head jerked upward; instinctively she retreated a step. He noted her reaction.

"Well you might!" he said softly. "What new nonsense is this?"

"I am going away," she said unnecessarily.

"So you were good enough to inform me in your very civil missive." He waved the letter under her nose. "You are mistaken, however. I am come to take you home."

"No, my lord."

"Do you come willingly?" he asked, as though she had not spoken. "Or must I use force?"

For once she sensed his resolution was greater than hers – and was confused. The color came and went in her face.

"Don't be idiotish!" she protested weakly. "You cannot mean to abduct me from so public a place!"

"Can I not?"

Several people were beginning to eye them curiously. The stage driver, her friend of last year, looked as though he would intervene.

Some of her old spirit returned. "And if I resist you , sir – summon assistance? What then?"

"Why, I shall explain that you have been turned off – and are attempting to abscond with the family silver. No one will care to doubt me, I think."

"Oh – you would do it, too!" she accused him with the ghost of a laugh ... and then in sudden panic, "Please, my lord! Let me go!"

"Never!" he declared vehemently. "I know how you feel about Tremaine, but it will pass. I will make you forget him!"

"Johnny?" Her bewilderment was apparent. "What has Johnny to do with it?"

His face went blank, and then began to warm.

Without a word, he lifted her into the curricle and tossed her belongings unceremoniously after her.

"My lord – Max – I can't!" she protested, laughing. "Mollie Patterson is expecting me."

"We'll send her a message by special courier," he said, dismissing the good lady with arrogant unconcern. "She will be the first to wish you happy. Come now ... you had best submit."

Free of the town the Earl pulled off the road. He removed Felicity's bonnet with fingers that shook slightly.

"Did you really suppose that I would let you go?" he demanded of her, and proceeded to demonstrate his ardor with the utmost thoroughness. "I should have done that days ago ... would have done if I hadn't returned from London to find young Tremaine practically sitting in your pocket! Lord knows, I had been wanting to ever since the night I assaulted you so disgracefully, my dearest love!"

"And I have been in an agony, convinced that you did not care!" Felicity chuckled softly. "We have made a sad botch of things between us!"

"Not any longer," he admonished. "I give you fair warning, I'll stand no nonsense about betrothals and bride clothes and the like! One such affair in the family will more than suffice! You shall have a mountain of clothes later, if you wish, but I have a special license burning a hole in my pocket at this very moment, and I intend to make use of it with indecent haste!"

"Do you?" Felicity stared, entranced.

"Then I shan't care a button even if I must stand up to be married in my shift! But, oh my dearest lord – are you quite sure?"

He demonstrated just how much, to her complete satisfaction.

"I shan't change my ways, you know," she prophesied, settling comfortably into his shoulder.

"I do know." He seemed undaunted by the prospect. "But it is my intention to keep you fully occupied. Since you are so good at managing children, I mean to provide you with a quiverful of your own."

Felicity gurgled irrepressibly. "Thank you, my lord! And I suppose you will arrange for all the boys to have the Delamere nose? And their father's charm?"

"Of course. And all the girls will have shining chestnut hair, and eyes that fizz when they are angry..." His intense scrutiny was making her blush. "...and betray their inmost feelings when they least realize it – as yours are doing at this very moment. And as for mouths," he murmured, warming to this theme...

"Max! The stage is coming..." In a panic, Felicity struggled to sit upright, but her lord was adamant and she finally submitted in laughing confusion.

The stage swept around the bend and bore down on them. As it flashed past, the outside passengers raised a spontaneous cheer, totally drowning the sole dissenter to comment sourly upon the Gentry's flagrant disregard for the sensibilities of others.

The driver grinned broadly and the guard, with a flourish, treated them to a final triumphant fanfare.

JOAN SMITH NOVELS
IN LARGE PRINT

An Affair Of The Heart

Aunt Sophie's Diamonds

Dame Durden's Daughter

Escapade

Imprudent Lady

La Comtesse

Sweet And Twenty

Clare Darcy Romances
in Large Print

Allegra

Cicily

Lydia

Victoire